Indigenous Novels, Indigenized Worlds

Indigenous Novels, Indigenized Worlds

Exploring the Indigenization of Fictional Worlds

Don K. Philpot

ROWMAN & LITTLEFIELD
Lanham • Boulder • New York • London

Published by Rowman & Littlefield
An imprint of The Rowman & Littlefield Publishing Group, Inc.
4501 Forbes Boulevard, Suite 200, Lanham, Maryland 20706
www.rowman.com

86-90 Paul Street, London EC2A 4NE, United Kingdom

British Library Cataloguing in Publication Information Available

Library of Congress Cataloging-in-Publication Data

Names: Philpot, Don K., author.
Title: Indigenous novels, indigenized worlds : exploring the indigenization of fictional worlds / Don K. Philpot.
Description: Lanham : Rowman & Littlefield, [2023] | Includes bibliographical references. | Summary: "Don K. Philpot offers teachers and students in intermediate and secondary grades an informative and well-articulated framework for exploring the experiences of Indigenous peoples in grade-level novels"—Provided by publisher.
Identifiers: LCCN 2023012659 (print) | LCCN 2023012660 (ebook) | ISBN 9781475860481 (cloth) | ISBN 9781475860498 (paperback) | ISBN 9781475860504 (epub)
Subjects: LCSH: Canadian fiction—Indian authors—History and criticism. | Children's stories, Canadian—History and criticism. | Indigenous peoples in literature.
Classification: LCC PR9188.2.I54 P45 2023 (print) | LCC PR9188.2.I54 (ebook) | DDC 813/.6099283—dc23/eng/20230524
LC record available at https://lccn.loc.gov/2023012659
LC ebook record available at https://lccn.loc.gov/2023012660

To the memory of McLeod and Alice George, who admitted me through their kindness, generosity, responsiveness, and love to the remarkable world of the Chemawawin Cree, past and present. Your teachings, personal histories, vision, joy, and resilience are always with me.

Contents

Prefatory Note About In-Text Citations and References

IN-TEXT CITATIONS

In this book, the middle and high school novels cited in chapters 3–9 are identified conveniently and for enhanced readability using titular acronyms. Acronyms and their corresponding book titles are shown below. Likewise for convenience and enhanced readability, page references in these same chapters are simply identified in parentheses.

BH	*Birchbark House*. Louise Erdrich. 1999.
COLH	*Children of the Longhouse*. Joseph Bruchac. 1996.
COTS	*The Curse of the Shaman*. Michael Kusugak. 2006.
DBDP	*Danny Blackgoat, Dangerous Passage*. Tim Tingle. 2017.
DBNP	*Danny Blackgoat, Navajo Prisoner*. Tim Tingle. 2013.
DBRRTF	*Danny Blackgoat, Rugged Road to Freedom*. Tim Tingle. 2014.
DP	*The Dark Pond*. Joseph Bruchac. 2002.
GOS	*The Game of Silence*. Louise Erdrich. 2005.
HR	*Hidden Roots*. Joseph Bruchac. 2004.
HTS	*Honor the Sun*. Ruby Slipperjack. 1987.
LLM	*Lana's Lakota Moons*. Virginia Driving Hawk Sneve. 2007.
LV	*Little Voice*. Ruby Slipperjack. 2001.
MT	*The Marrow Thieves*. Cherie Dimaline. 2017.
MTTT	*March Toward the Thunder*. Joseph Bruchac. 2008.
NMNN	*No More No Name*. Tim Tingle. 2017.
NN	*No Name*. Tim Tingle. 2014.

SM	*Skeleton Man*. Joseph Bruchac. 2001.
SRC	*Stone River Crossing*. Tim Tingle. 2019.
SW	*Silent Words*. Ruby Slipperjack. 1992.
TPY	*The Porcupine Year*. Louise Erdrich. 2008.
WG	*Will's Garden*. Lee Maracle. 2002.
WIB	*Where I Belong*. Tara White. 2014.
WITD	*Whisper in the Dark*. Joseph Bruchac. 2005.
WP	*The Winter People*. Joseph Bruchac. 2002.

REFERENCES

In this book, bibliographic details for all the books above are provided in chapters 1 and 2. These 24 novels are main sources of information about indigenizing features in fictional worlds. Bibliographic details for additional sources of information used in this book appear at the end of applicable chapters.

Chapter 1

Indigenous Novels, Indigenized Worlds

In Canada and the United States, an increasing number of novels written for young people ages 10–16—by Indigenous authors—present fictional worlds that are deliberately indigenized. Indigenized fictional worlds, as in the historical novel *The Porcupine Year* (Erdrich 2008) and the contemporary realistic novel *Will's Garden* (Maracle 2002), explicitly focus on the personal experiences of one or two young people who are members of an identified Indigenous group and inhabit a landscape that is largely dominated by Indigenous people.

The indigenized fictional worlds presented in *The Porcupine Year* (Erdrich 2008) and *Will's Garden* (Maracle 2002) are largely populated by Sto: loh and Anishinabe (Ojibwe) people and focus on the personal experiences of a 12-year-old girl Omakayas in the first novel and a 16-year-old boy Will in the second. Will lives with his parents and siblings on Cheam First Nation lands in the Upper Fraser Valley region of British Columbia. Omakayas was born in the 1840s and lives with her Anishinabe parents, grandmother, siblings, and other relatives on the Island of the Golden-Breasted Woodpecker in Lake Superior.

Through the fictional worlds they indigenize for readers ages 10–16, Indigenous authors like Louise Erdrich and Lee Maracle provide unique access to the lived experiences of Indigenous people, past, present, or future and the worlds they inhabit. Both Indigenous and non-Indigenous readers can learn substantially about Indigenous people and themselves through sustained immersion in fictional worlds where Indigenous people are foregrounded, active, autonomous, respected, and valued.

This book seeks to understand the substantive and specific ways Indigenous authors indigenize the fictional worlds they create and present in novels for readers ages 10–16. But rather than focusing on Indigenous authors and their methodologies, this book focuses instead on the fictional worlds themselves and explicitly identifiable textual features that produce indigenized worlds.

INDIGENOUS NOVELS, INDIGENIZED WORLDS

Indigenous Peoples, Indigenous Novels, Indigenized Worlds

The government of Canada (2022) uses the term *Indigenous peoples* as a collective name for the original (first) peoples of North America and their descendants. In the United States, the first peoples are popularly referred to as Native Americans. For the purpose of this book, the term *Indigenous peoples* is used as a collective name for all first peoples of the United States and Canada and their descendants, and the terms *Indigenous people* and *Indigenous person* are used respectively to identify a specific Indigenous group (e.g., Anishnaabe, Sto: loh, Choctaw, Navajo) or an individual member of an Indigenous group.

An Indigenous novel is a fictional narrative published in the form of a novel that is written by an Indigenous person and focuses on one or more fictional individuals that belong to an Indigenous group. A fictional world is indigenized when the personal experiences of its prominent inhabitants substantively align with the experiences of Indigenous peoples.

Twelve Categories of Indigenizing Features

A close analysis of 24 Indigenous novels—originally published in Canada or the United States and written for readers ages 10–16—revealed more than 150 indigenizing features. These features are organized into primary and secondary groups: Groups A–D and Categories 1–12 respectively. Group A includes three Categories, Group B four Categories, Group C two Categories, and Group D three Categories.

The number of indigenizing features included in each Category ranges from 3 (Category 2 Tribal History) to 40 (Category 7 Traditions). Sample indigenizing features in each primary grouping Group A–D appear below. The methodology used in the analysis and organization of indigenizing features is discussed in the next chapter.

Group A (1–3). Time, Tribal History, Ancestry (12 features)
Sample features: seasonal habitation cycles, notable people, ancestral
    beings

Group B (4–7). Cultural Beliefs, Values, Events, Traditions (81 features)
Sample features: visions, expressing gratitude, naming feasts, traditional houses

Group C (8–9). Language Use, Stories, Storytelling, Family Life, Kinship (28 features)
Sample features: stories about culture heroes, kinship with local animals

Group D (10–12). Destruction and Restoration (37 features)
Sample features: forced relocation from homeland, sovereignty, recovery

Two Indigenous Novels, Briefly: Indigenizing Features

Indigenizing features from all Groups A–D are present in the two novels named at the start of this chapter: *The Porcupine Year* (Erdrich 2008) and *Will's Garden* (Maracle 2002). Not surprisingly, however, the fictional world in each of these novels is indigenized in a distinctive way. A comprehensive inventory of indigenizing features for these novels yields two distinctive patterns of features.

The fictional worlds in both novels are indigenized by features in the Categories of Time, Ancestry, Cultural Beliefs, Cultural Practices, Cultural Events, Cultural Traditions, Language Use, Stories, Storytelling, Family Life, Kinship, Divestment or Denigration, and Leadership. Neither fictional world is indigenized by features in the Category of Tribal History, and the fictional world in *Will's Garden* (Maracle 2002) is not indigenized by features in the Categories of Cultural Values, Restoration, or Recovery.

Individual indigenizing features common to both novels include ancestral lands and ancestral identity (3. Ancestry); praying and prayers, sacred offerings, and sacred objects (4. Religious Beliefs and Practices); traditional songs and singing (6. Cultural Events); fishing and traditional foods (7. Traditions); family stories (8. Language Use, Stories, and Storytelling); and elders (11. Sovereignty, Defense, Leadership). An inventory of features for each novel is shown summatively below. These summative inventories are preceded by bibliographic details and a publisher summary for each novel.

Erdrich, Louise. 2008. *The Porcupine Year.* New York: HarperCollins. Hardcover. 193 pages. 16 chapters. Includes an author's note, glossary, and additional notes and a map. Illustrated. Historical fiction. Middle grade novel. Lexile Measure 840L.

Story details from front flap. Here follows the story of a most extraordinary year in the life of an Ojibwe family and of a girl named "Omakayas," or Little Frog, who lived a year of flight and adventure, pain and joy, in 1852.

When Omakayas is twelve winters old, she and her family set off on a harrowing journey. They travel by canoe westward from the shores of Lake Superior along the rivers of northern Minnesota, in search of a new home. While the family has prepared well, unexpected danger, enemies, and hardships will push them to the brink of survival. Omakayas continues to learn from the land and the spirits around her, and she discovers that no matter where she is, or how she is living, she has the one thing she needs to carry her through.

Group A (1–3). Time, Tribal History, Ancestry (4/12 features)
Features: seasonal habitation cycles; ancestral lands, ancestral identity, ancestral beings

Group B (4–7). Cultural Beliefs, Values, Events, Traditions (35/81 features)
Sample features: beliefs about the Creator, spirit helpers, guides, protectors, praying and prayers, sacred offerings, sacred songs, sacred objects, sacred drums and drumming, honoring the dead, purification practices; valuing dreams, acting calmly, humbly, and honorably; traditional songs and singing, naming feasts, Indigenous coming-of-age ceremony; traditional knowledge about local wildlife, traditional roles, large game hunting, rabbit hunting, bird hunting, trapping, fishing, plant and wild rice harvesting, water travel, snow travel, traditional shelters, house and shelter building, traditional clothing accessories, blankets and blanket making, traditional implements, traditional foods, traditional drinks, food preparation, food storage

Group C (8–9). Language, Storytelling, Family Life, Kinship (10/28 features)
Sample features: ancestral language, names and naming, storytelling time, stories about culture heroes, stories about legendary individuals, personal stories, family stories; extended family households, sibling avoidance, childhood play

Group D (10–12). Destruction, Sovereignty, Restoration (6/37 features)
Sample features: material appropriation, forced relocation from homeland, smallpox, elders, recovery, restoration

Maracle, Lee. 2002. *Will's Garden*. Penticton, BC: Theytus. Paperback. 194 pages. 18 chapters. Not illustrated. Contemporary realistic fiction. Secondary grade novel. Not leveled.

Story details from back cover. As Will is preparing for his coming-of-age ceremony, the whole family teams together, working day and night to prepare. Meanwhile life goes on at school in relationships and with friends. When a gang of jocks try to overpower the weaker nerds at school, Will steps up and confronts the real issues of power struggles, racism, homophobia, bullying, and name calling.

As ceremony time draws nearer, Will becomes infatuated with the idea of love and long-term relationships. A sudden and serious illness gives him time to reflect over what he's learned about becoming a man, the women in this life, and consider his future as a Sto: loh caretaker of the land in the modern world.

Group A (1–3). Time, Tribal History, Ancestry (3/12 features)
Sample features: dreamtime, ancestral lands, ancestral identity

Group B (4–7). Cultural Beliefs, Values, Events, Traditions (14/81 features)
Sample features: praying and prayers, sacred offerings, sacred objects, sacred drums and drumming; stationary games, grass dance, fancy dance, traditional songs and singing, Sto: loh becoming man ceremony; fishing, clamming, wood carving, beadwork and quillwork, traditional foods

Group C (8–9). Language-Storytelling; Family Life-Kinship (7/28 features)
Sample features: art of storytelling, stories about animal tricksters, eagle stories, family stories, Indigenous writing; courtship, clan membership

Group D (10–12). Destruction, Sovereignty, Restoration (3/37 features)
Sample features: cultural denigration; chiefs, elders

INDIGENOUS AUTHORS, INDIGENOUS NOVELS, AND NARRATIVE GENRE

This book focuses exclusively on Indigenous novels aimed at readers ages 10–16. The 24 novels selected for this book were written by Joseph Bruchac, Virginia Driving Hawk Sneve, Cherie Dimaline, Louise Erdrich, Lee Maracle, Ruby Slipperjack, Michael Kusugak, Tim Tingle, and Tara White. The publication dates for these novels range from 1988 to 2019. Ten novels are classified as historical novels, nine as contemporary realistic novels, and five as fantasy novels.

BOOK ORGANIZATION AND CHAPTER OVERVIEWS

The book is organized into two sections. Part I includes the present chapter along with chapter 2 whose content, taken together, prepares readers for the detailed discussion and illustration of distinctive indigenizing features in Part II.

Part I: Indigenized Worlds, Indigenous Worldviews

Chapter 1 provided a brief introduction to the narrative phenomenon of fictional worlds and specific features that distinguish Indigenous worlds from other fictional worlds presented in novels for readers ages 10–16. As reported in this chapter, more than 150 distinctive indigenizing features spanning 12 categories were identified in an analysis of 24 Indigenous novels for young people. The chapter also presented snapshot views of indigenizing features in two of the 24 novels explored in this book.

Chapter 2 presents the set of criteria used to select 24 Indigenous novels for the exploration of indigenizing fictional world features. It also presents details about each novel selected and biographical information about the authors of these books. The chapter ends with a brief discussion of the methodology used in this book to analyze fictional worlds.

Part II: Distinctive Features of Indigenized Worlds

The seven chapters in Part II present summatively as a group a comprehensive inventory of features that distinguishes the fictional worlds in the 24 novels examined in this book. Each feature is illustrated by an example from one or more novels.

Chapters 3–6 focus on the first two groups of indigenizing features: Groups A and B. Chapter 3 focuses exclusively on Group A features: Time, Tribal History, and Ancestry. Chapters 4–6 focus on Group B features. Chapter 4 focuses on Cultural Beliefs, chapter 5 Cultural Values and Events, and chapter 6 Cultural Traditions.

Chapters 7–9 focus on the last two groups of indigenizing features, Group C and D. Chapter 7 focuses on the Group C features of Language, Stories, and Storytelling and chapter 8 the Group C features of Family Life and Kinship. Chapter 9, the final chapter in the book, focuses exclusively on Group D features: Destruction, Sovereignty, and Restoration.

Two helpful resources appear at the end of the book. An inventory of features template appears in appendix A. Readers may use this template to complete their own inventory of indigenizing features for novels by Indigenous authors not examined in this book.

A comprehensive inventory of indigenizing features for each novel named first in this book, *The Porcupine Year* (Erdrich 2008) and *Will's Garden* (Maracle 2002), appears in appendix B. Together the two appendices will assist readers in their envisioning and appreciation of the full set of indigenizing features which yields the distinctive fictional world presented in each novel.

INDIGENIZED FICTIONAL WORLDS: BOOKS 1 AND 2

Two Books: A Complementary Focus

This book is one of two that focus on Indigenous novels and indigenized fictional worlds. The essential question addressed in this first book focuses on indigenizing features, and the essential question addressed in the second book focuses on classroom explorations of indigenized worlds with students in grades 5–10. Essential Question 1: What features in Indigenous middle and secondary grade novels yield indigenized fictional worlds? Essential Question 2: What new and transformative understandings about Indigenous peoples in the United States and Canada can young people gain from classroom explorations of Indigenous novels and indigenized worlds?

Essential question 1 is answered in this first book by an analysis of 24 Indigenous novels and the delineation—identification and description—of specific textual features that produce indigenized fictional worlds. Essential Question 2 will be answered by teachers and students in grades 5–10 through collaborative classroom explorations of indigenized fictional worlds using the framework of features offered by this first book and additional complementary resources offered by the second.

Intended Readers

Both books are primarily intended for teachers in grades 5–10, in-service teachers, pre-service teachers, and teacher educators with specializations in English language arts, social studies, history, and Indigenous Studies. The first book will also interest students and scholars in the fields of English Literature, Children's Literature, Adolescent Literature, World Literature, and Indigenous Studies.

This first book has many distinctive offerings which will make it a valuable resource for a broad group of readers, offerings that include:

- a sustained focus on novels for middle and secondary grade students written by contemporary Indigenous writers
- a highly readable and diverse set of novels which represent all major novel genres (historical, realistic, fantasy)
- highly engaging novels that feature a broad range of North American Indigenous characters and cultures in different geographic and temporal settings
- highly relevant content for students in grades 5–10
- a highly useable framework for exploring Indigenous novels

REFERENCES

Government of Canada (2022). "Indigenous peoples and communities." *Crown-Indigenous Relations and Northern Affairs Canada (RCAANC)*. February 4, 2023. https://www.rcaanc-cirnac.gc.ca/eng/1100100013785/1529102490303.

Chapter 2

Indigenous Novels and Novelists

CHAPTER OVERVIEW

This chapter has a four-part focus. It identifies a set of criteria that was used to select appropriate novels for a book-length study of indigenizing fictional world features, provides information about each selected novel and its author, and describes the methodology used to analyze fictional worlds in terms of indigenizing features.

SELECTED NOVELS

Novel Selection Criteria

Twenty-four novels were selected for this book's analysis of indigenizing fictional world features. All 24 novels selected were (1) written by Indigenous (2) American or Canadian authors; and all but one (the first book in the *Birchbark House* series) (3) focus on the personal experiences of an Indigenous young person (4) age 10–16. All 24 novels (5) were published by mainstream American or Canadian publishing companies (6) as novels and more specifically as (7) contemporary realistic, historical, or fantasy novels, (8) primarily intended for readers age 10–16.

Showcased Worlds, Individuals, and Cultures

A diverse group of fictional young people are reflected in the selected set of novels. Twelve novels focus on the personal experiences of boys age 10–16, eleven on girls age 10–14, one on a twin brother and sister age 11, and one on a girl age 8.

This diverse group of Indigenous young people live in different parts of the United States and Canada at different points in time, and belong to distinctive Indigenous communities and cultures including the Anishinaabe Nation (Ojibwe), Kanien'kehá:ka Nation (Mohawk), Dine Nation (Navajo), Wabanaki Nation (Abenaki), Lakota Nation (Sioux), Sto: lo Nation (Salish), Narragansett Nation, or Shawnee Nation.

Annotated References and Story Descriptions

An annotated reference and brief story description from the back cover or inner flaps for each novel follows. The story descriptions provide personal and cultural contexts for this book-length study of Indigenous novels and indigenized worlds.

> Bruchac, Joseph. 1996. *Children of the Longhouse.* New York: Dial. Hardcover. 150 pages. 13 chapters and epilogue. Includes an afterword, suggested readings, and glossary. Not illustrated. Historical fiction. Middle grade novel. Guided Reading Level S. Lexile Measure 950L.

Story details from front flap. In this gripping novel set in a Mohawk village of the late 1400s, eleven-year-old twins are caught up against their will in a dangerous rivalry with a gang of older boys.

At eleven winters, strong, courageous Ohkwa'ri and his thoughtful twin sister Otsi:stia are among the most admired young people in their village. Yet the older boy called Grabber has no love for the twins, and when Ohkwa'ri tells the clan leaders of Grabber's foolhardy plan to raid another village, he makes a powerful enemy.

Ohkwa'ri excels at Tekwaarathon, the sport that centuries later would be known as lacrosse. He is thrilled when a big ball game involving all the men of the village is announced—until he realizes that Grabber and his friends will be looking for any chance to hurt him. Ohkwa'ri believes in the path of peace, but can peaceful ways prevail against Grabber's wrath?

> Bruchac, Joseph. 2001. *Skeleton Man.* New York: Harper Trophy. Hardcover. 114 pages. 16 chapters. Illustrated. Fantasy fiction (ghost story). Middle grade novel. Guided Reading Level V. Lexile Measure 730L.

Story details from back cover. Ever since the morning Molly woke up to find that her parents had vanished, her life has become filled with terrible questions. Where have her parents gone? Who is this spooky old man who's taken her to live with him, claiming to be her great-uncle? Why does he never eat, and why does he lock her in her room at night? What are her dreams of the

Skeleton Man trying to tell her? There's one thing Molly does know. She needs to find some answers before it's too late.

Bruchac, Joseph. 2002. *The Winter People*. New York: Dial. Hardcover. 168 pages. 29 chapters. Includes an author's note. Not illustrated. Historical fiction. Grades 7–10 novel. Guided Reading Level X. Lexile Measure 800L.

Story details from front flap. Saxso is fourteen when the British attack his village. It's 1759, and war is raging in the northeast between the British and the French, with the Abenaki people—Saxso's people—by their side. Without enough warriors to defend their homes, Saxso's village is burned to the ground. Many people are killed, but some, including Saxso's mother and two sisters, are taken hostage. Now it's up to Saxso, on his own, to track the raiders and bring his family back home . . . before it's too late.

Bruchac, Joseph. 2002. *The Dark Pond*. New York: HarperTrophy. Paperback. 142 pages. 11 chapters. Illustrated. Fantasy fiction (ghost story). Middle grade novel. Guided Reading Level not available. Lexile Measure 820L.

Story details from back cover. As soon as he arrived at the North Mountains School, Armie senses something strange about the dark pond in the forest. An eerie presence haunts his dreams and keeps drawing him back to the pond— something dangerous that lurks in its depths. Armie turns to the tales of his Shawnee ancestors for help—but if he's right about what lives in the still, black waters of the dark pond, he may need more than his wits to survive.

Bruchac, Joseph. 2004. *Hidden Roots*. New York: Scholastic. Hardcover. 136 pages. 15 chapters. Includes an author's note. Not illustrated. Contemporary realistic fiction. Middle grade novel. Guided Reading Level not available. Lexile Measure 830L.

Story details from front flap. As hard as they try, 11-year-old Sonny and his mother can't predict his father's sudden rages, which can turn physical in an instant. Jake's anger only gets worse after long days laboring at the local paper mill—and when Uncle Louis appears. Louis seems to show up when Sonny and his mother need help most, but there is something about him and his quiet, wise ways that only fuels Jake's rage. The love of Sonny's fragile mother, the support and protection of his Uncle Louis, and an unexpected friendship with a librarian help Sonny gain the confidence to stand up to his father. The consequences of his actions, and the source of his father's self-hatred, will reverberate through the hearts and minds of readers and challenge them to examine their own feelings about love, acceptance, and self-esteem.

Bruchac, Joseph. 2005. *Whisper in the Dark.* New York: Dial. Paperback. 174 pages. 27 chapters. Illustrated. Fantasy fiction (ghost story). Middle grade novel. Guided Reading Level not available. Lexile Measure 870L.

Story details from back cover. Maddy has always loved scary stories, especially the spooky legends of her Native American ancestors. But that was before she heard about the Whisperer in the Dark, the most frightening legend of all. Now there's an icy voice at the other end of the phone and a terrifying message left on Maddy's door. Suddenly this ancient tale is becoming just a bit too real. Once, twice, three times he's called out to her. If he calls to her a fourth time, she's done for. Where will she be when he calls her name again?

Bruchac, Joseph. 2008. *March Toward the Thunder.* New York: Dial Books. Hardcover. 298 pages. 36 chapters. Includes fore and end matter. Illustrated. Historical fiction. Middle grade novel. Guided Reading Level Z. Lexile Measure 850L.

Story details from front flap. Louis Nolette is not American or Irish; he's an Abenaki Indian from Canada. He's also just fifteen years old. But none of this stops him from joining the Fighting 69th, the Irish Brigade known for its courage and ferocity in battle. During the final years of the Civil War, Louis feels compelled to join up by the North's commitment to end slavery as well as the promise of good wages. But war is never what you expect, and as he fights in battle after battle, including Cold Harbor, the Wilderness, and the Crater, Louis discovers prejudice and acceptance, courage and cowardice in the most surprising places.

Dimaline, Cherie 2017. *The Marrow Thieves.* Toronto: DBC. Paperback. 231 pages. 27 chapters. Not illustrated. Fantasy fiction. Grades 8–12 novel. Guided Reading Level not available. Lexile Measure 810L.

Story details from back cover. Just when you think you have nothing left to lose, they come for your dreams. In a world nearly destroyed by global warming, the Indigenous people of North America are being hunted for their bone marrow, which carries the key to recovering something the rest of the population has lost: the ability to dream. Frenchie and his companions, struggling to survive, don't yet know that one of them holds the secret to defeating the marrow thieves.

Driving Hawk Sneve, Virginia. 2007. *Lana's Lakota Moons.* Lincoln, NE: University of Nebraska Press. Paperback. 116 pages. 12 chapters. Not illustrated. Contemporary realistic fiction. Grades 7–10 novel. Not leveled.

Story details from front flap. Lori is a quiet, contemplative bookworm. Lana is an outspoken adventuress. Different as they are, they are first cousins, sisters in the Lakota way. And when both befriend a Hmong girl new to their school, the discovery of a culture so strange to them and so rich with possibilities brings them together as never before in an experience of life and loss. As the girls learn of the moons of the Lakota calendar, they also learn that the circle of life is never broken, even when death comes to one of them.

Erdrich, Louise. 1999. *Birchbark House.* New York: Hyperion. Paperback. 244 pages. 14 chapters. Includes an author's note and glossary. Illustrated. Historical fiction. Middle grade novel. Guided Reading Level T. Lexile Measure 970L.

Story details from back cover. Omakayas and her family live on the land her people call the Island of the Golden-Breasted Woodpecker. Although the "chimookoman," white people, encroach more and more on their land, life continues much as it always has: every summer they build a new birchbark house; every fall they go to their ricing camp to harvest and feast; they move to the cedar log house before the first snows arrive, and celebrate the end of the long, cold winters at their maple-sugaring camp. In between, Omakayas fights with her annoying little brother, Pinch; plays with the adorable baby, Neewo; and tries to be grown-up like her big sister, Angeline. But the satisfying rhythms of their life are shattered when a visitor comes to their lodge one winter night, bringing with him an invisible enemy that will change things forever—but that will eventually lead Omakayas to discover her calling.

Erdrich, Louise. 2005. *The Game of Silence.* New York: HarperCollins. Hardcover. 256 pages. 16 chapters. Includes an author's note, glossary, and additional notes. Illustrated. Historical fiction. Middle grade novel. Lexile Measure 900L.

Story details from front flap. Her name is Omakayas, or Little Frog, because her first step was a hop, and she lives on an island in Lake Superior. It is 1850, and the lives of the Ojibwe have returned to a familiar rhythm: they build their birchbark houses in the summer, go to the ricing camps in the fall to harvest and feast, and move to their cozy cedar log cabins near the town of

LaPointe before the first snows. The satisfying routines of Omakayas's days are interrupted by a surprise visit from a group of desperate and mysterious people. From them, she learns that all their lives may drastically change. The chimookomanag, or white people, want Omakayas and her people to leave their island in Lake Superior and move farther west. Omakayas realizes that something so valuable, so important that she never knew she had it in the first place, is in danger: her home. Her way of life.

Kusugak, Michael. 2006. *The Curse of the Shaman*. Toronto: Harper Trophy Canada. Paperback. 158 pages. 23 chapters. Includes an afterword. Illustrated. Fantasy fiction (literary legend). Grades 6–10 novel. Not leveled.

Story details from back cover. Sometimes even shamans get cranky. That was baby Wolverine's misfortune—to be cursed by an out-of-sorts shaman frustrated by his own baby daughter's incessant crying. Not only has shaman Paaliaq forbidden the future marriage of Wolverine to Breath, Paaliaq's beautiful but teary baby girl, he has cursed Wolverine, banishing him when he becomes a young man. And even when a contrite Paaliaq later revokes the curse, the shaman's even crankier magic animal will not. Now Wolverine finds himself stranded on a barren island, locked in a life-or-death struggle to return to his home, his family, and a very special young girl.

Slipperjack, Ruby. 1987. *Honour the Sun*. Saskatoon: Fifth House Publishers. Hardcover. 211 pages. 27 chapters. Not illustrated. Contemporary realistic fiction. Grades 6–10 novel. Not leveled.

Story details from back cover. In northern Ontario, dotted along the C.N.R. line, are many small, isolated, Native communities. A long time ago, some of them had been trading posts and had attracted past generations of Indian people from different reserves. Among them were those people who had intermarried and had never returned to their respective reserves. In *Honour the Sun*, Ruby Slipperjack creates one such community where her character, a ten-year-old girl called The Owl, writes seasonal diaries, beginning in the summer of 1962. She writes of the warm, moving, carefree, often humorous events of her childhood. Upon reaching her teen years, The Owl feels the first sorrow as an ominous climate of change seems to overwhelm her circle of friends, and then, a deep despair, as it includes even her mother, once her source of strength and security. With helpless frustration, she watches, unable to understand why her mother seems to suddenly succumb to alcohol. As a sixteen-year-old who has had to leave her community for further schooling, she returns for a summer visit, and realizes that despite all the changes, despite the alienation, her mother's words will always be with her: "Honour the Sun, child. Just as it comes over the horizon, honour the Sun, that it may bless you, come another day . . ."

Slipperjack, Ruby. 1992. *Silent Words.* Saskatoon: Fifth House Publishers. Hardcover. 250 pages. 20 chapters and epilogue. Not illustrated. Contemporary realistic fiction. Grades 7–10 novel. Not leveled.

Story details from back cover. Set in northwestern Ontario in the 1960s, *Silent Words* tells the story of a young Native boy and his journey of self-discovery. Danny's life is a daily struggle for survival. He runs away from his violent and abusive home and, on his own, finds his way through a series of Native communities along the CN mainline. Various people take the boy in for a time, including a family with other children, an elderly couple, a boy and his father, a young bachelor, and a wise old man. Through his travels and encounters, Danny learns about himself and the world he lives in.

Slipperjack, Ruby. 2001. *Little Voice.* Regina: Coteau Books. Paperback. 246 pages. 13 chapters. Illustrated. Contemporary realistic fiction. Grades 6–10 novel. Not leveled.

Story details from back cover. Kids make fun of her green eyes. And she's got a boy's name. Ray just doesn't fit in. Life's been tough for Ray since her father died in a logging accident. Kids at school make fun of her. She misses her dad very much, and she thinks her mother is too busy to need her. Things get so bad, she almost stops talking. Then Ray gets the chance she's always wanted: to spend the summer with her grandma, an elder and healer in a northern Ontario community. Helping Grandma—canoeing, camping, fishing, berry picking—Ray begins to learn a new way of life. Grandma's wisdom, love, and humor help Ray to understand herself better. Ray discovers that learning in two different ways—from her grandma's traditional teachings and from school—can prepare her for a very special life, and help her to find her own voice.

Tingle, Tim. 2014. *No Name.* Summertown, TN: 7th Generation. Paperback. 160 pages. 21 chapters. Not illustrated. Contemporary realistic fiction. Grades 7–10 novel. Not leveled.

Story details from publisher's website. Inspired by the traditional Choctaw story "No Name," this modern adaptation features a present-day Choctaw teenager surviving tough family times. Abandoned by his mother, Bobby Byington is left alone with his mean-spirited, abusive father. The one place the teen can find peace is on the neighborhood basketball court. But after a violent confrontation with his father, the teen runs away, only to return home to find an unexpected hiding spot in his own backyard that becomes his home for weeks. When Bobby has a chance to play on the high school basketball team, he decides—with the help and encouragement of his coach, a Cherokee buddy, and a quiet next-door girlfriend—to face his father.

Tingle, Tim. 2017. *No More No Name.* Summertown, TN: 7th Generation. Paperback. 161 pages. 21 chapters. Not illustrated. Contemporary realistic fiction. Grades 7–10 novel. Not leveled.

Story details from publisher's website. In *No Name*, the first book in the series, Bobby Byington has to navigate his father's alcoholism and anger, but in *No More No Name*, life is looking up. Bobby is learning to trust his alcohol-free father and is finally able to return to his beloved game of basketball. But off the court is a different matter. New problems surface when Bobby's smart girlfriend is bullied by a resentful schoolmate and a fellow team member is abused by his own alcoholic father. With the confidence Bobby learned from the Choctaw legend "No Name," he is determined to find a way to help his friends.

Tingle, Tim. 2013. *Danny Blackgoat, Navajo Prisoner.* 7th Generation. Paperback. 151 pages. 17 chapters. Includes an author's note. Not illustrated. Historical fiction. Grades 7–10 novel. Not leveled.

Story details from publisher's website. Danny Blackgoat is a teenager in Navajo country when United States soldiers burn down his home, kill his sheep, capture his family. They are forced, along with other captured Navajo, to march on the Navajo Long Walk of 1864. During the journey, Danny is labeled a troublemaker and given the name Fire Eye. Refusing to accept captivity, he is sent to Fort Davis, Texas, a Civil War prisoner outpost. There he battles bullying fellow prisoners, rattlesnakes, and abusive soldiers, until he meets Jim Davis. Davis teaches Danny how to hold his anger and starts him on the road to literacy. In a stunning climax, Davis—who builds coffins for the dead—aids Danny in a daring and dangerous escape. Set in troubled times, *Danny Blackgoat, Navajo Prisoner* is the story of one boy's hunger to be free and to be Navajo.

Tingle, Tim. 2014. *Danny Blackgoat, Rugged Road to Freedom.* 7th Generation. Paperback. 163 pages. 21 chapters. Not illustrated. Historical fiction. Grades 7–10 novel. Not leveled.

Story details from publisher's website. This second volume of the trilogy continues the dramatic story of Danny Blackgoat, a Navajo teenager who, after being labeled a troublemaker on the Long Walk of 1864, is separated from his family. After a daring escape from prison in the first volume, in this second volume Danny must face many dangerous obstacles in his effort to rescue his family and find freedom. Whether it's soldiers and bandits chasing him or the dangers of the harsh desert climate, Danny ricochets from one bad situation to the next, but his bravery doesn't falter and he never loses faith.

Tingle, Tim. 2017. *Danny Blackgoat, Dangerous Passage.* 7th Generation. Paperback. 162 pages. 22 chapters. Includes an afterword and recommended resources. Not illustrated. Historical fiction. Grades 7–10 novel. Not leveled.

Story details from publisher's website. Suspected horse thief Danny Blackgoat narrowly escapes capture by the authorities as he makes the dangerous journey to reunite with his family being held in prison. Along his route, Danny helps old friends, continues to dodge capture, and falls in love. As he nears his destination, he knows he must be very diligent to avoid danger but when Danny is told his beloved friend Jim Davis is charged with the horse theft, Danny surrenders. Now the fate of both men lies in the balance between the hangman's noose and an unlikely turn of events.

Tingle, Tim. 2019. *Stone River Crossing.* New York: Tu Books. Hardcover. 325 pages. 51 chapters. Includes a glossary and author's note. Not illustrated. Historical fiction. Grades 6–10 novel. Not leveled.

Story details from back cover. Martha Tom knows better than to cross the Bok Chitto River to pick blackberries. The Bok Chitto is the only border between her town in the Choctaw Nation and the slave-owning plantation in Mississippi territory. The slave owners could catch her, too. What was she thinking? But crossing the river brings a surprise friendship with Lil Mo, a boy who is enslaved on the other side. Lil Mo discovers that his mother is about to be sold and the rest of his family left behind. But Martha Tom has the answer: cross the Bok Chitto and become free.

Crossing to freedom with his family seems impossible with slave catchers roaming, but then there is a miracle—a magical night where things become unseen and souls walk on water. By morning, Lil Mo discovers he has entered a completely new world of tradition, community, and . . . a little magic. But as Lil Mo's family adjusts to their new life, danger waits just around the corner.

White, Tara. 2014. *Where I Belong.* Vancouver: Tradewind Books. Paperback. 109 pages. 15 chapters. Not illustrated. Contemporary realistic fiction. Grades 7–10 novel. Not leveled.

Story details from back cover. This moving tale of self-discovery takes place during the Oka uprising in the summer of 1990. Adopted as an infant, Carrie has always felt somehow out of place. Recurring dreams haunt her, warning her that someone close to her is in danger. When she discovers that her birth family is Mohawk living in Quebec, she makes the long journey and finally achieves the sense of home and belonging that had always eluded her.

SHOWCASED NOVELISTS

Bruchac, Joseph (Abenaki, United States)

Joseph Bruchac is an Abenaki writer and storyteller. To date, he has published over 120 books for children and adults. His books for children include picture books, short stories, traditional stories, biographies, and novels.

Bruchac's novels for younger readers, ages 10–12, include *Children of the Longhouse* (1996), *Eagle Song* (1997), *Heart of a Chief* (1998), *Skeleton Man* (2001), *The Journal of Jesse Smoke* (2001), *Arrow Over the Door* (2002), *Hidden Roots* (2004), *The Warriors* (2004), *Dark Pond* (2004), *Whisper in the Dark* (2005), *Wabi: A Hero's Tale* (2006), *Return of Skeleton Man* (2006), *Bear Walker* (2007), *Dragon Castle* (2011), and *Rez Dogs* (2022).

Bruchac's novels for older readers, ages 13–16, include *Winter People* (2002), *Code Talker* (2005), *The Way* (2007), *March Toward the Thunder* (2009), *Wolf Park* (2011), *Trail of the Dead* (2015), *Rose Eagle* (2014), *Long Run* (2016), *Talking Leaves* (2017), *Killer of Enemies* (2017), *Night Wings* (2018), *Two Roads* (2019), *Found* (2020), *Arrow of Lightning* (2021), and *Peacemaker* (2022).

Bruchac holds a bachelor's degree from Cornell University, a master's degree in Literature and Creative Writing from Syracuse University, and a doctorate in Comparative Literature from the Union Institute and University of Ohio. In 1999, Bruchac received the Lifetime Achievement Award from the Native Writers' Circle of the Americas.

Dimaline, Cherie (Metis, Canada)

Cherie Dimaline is a member of the Georgian Bay (Ontario) Métis Nation on Lake Huron. Her published works for adults include novels, collections of short stories, individual short stories, and magazine articles. In 2013, she was founding editor of *Muskrat Magazine*, an online Indigenous arts and culture magazine. In 2014, she was selected as the Emerging Artist of the Year at the Ontario Premier's Awards for Excellence in Arts, and in 2015 served as writer in residence at Toronto Public Library.

The *Marrow Thieves* (2017) is Dimaline's first novel for young people. The novel received two national literary awards in Canada: the Governor General's Award for Young People's Literature (2017) and the Burt Award for First Nations, Inuit and Métis Young Adult Literature (2018). Dimaline currently lives in Toronto.

Driving Hawk Sneve, Virginia (Sicangu Lakota, United States)

Virginia Driving Hawk Sneve is a member of the Rosebud Sioux Tribe (Sicangu Lakota Oyate or Burnt Thigh Nation). In her long career as a teacher and writer, Sneve has written more than 20 books, fiction and nonfiction, for children and adults. In 1972, she published two novels for young people: *Jimmy Yellow Hawk* and *High Elk's Treasure*. Her other novels for young people include *When Thunders Spoke* (1974), *The Chichi Hoohoo Bogeyman* (1993), *The Trickster and the Troll* (1997), and *Lana's Lakota Moons* (2007).

Sneve was born in 1933 and grew up on the Rosebud Indian Reservation in South Dakota. She earned a high school diploma from St. Mary's School for Indian Girls in Springfield, South Dakota and undergraduate and graduate degrees from South Dakota State University in 1954 and 1969 respectively. In 1979 she received an Honorary Doctorate of Letters from Dakota Wesleyan University and in 2000 was awarded the National Humanities Medal for her literary efforts by President Clinton.

Erdrich, Louise (Anishinaabe, United States)

Louise Erdrich is a member of the Turtle Mountain Band of Chippewa Indians in North Dakota. Her books for children and adults, including her series of five *Birchbark House* novels for children ages 8–12, have earned her international acclaim as an American writer. Erdrich published her first novel for adults in 1984 and her first work of fiction for children, a picture book, in 1996.

Erdrich's *Birchbark House* series for children includes *The Birchbark House* (1999), *Game of Silence* (2005), *The Porcupine Year* (2008), *Chickadee* (2012), and *Makoons* (2016). Two novels in the series, *Game of Silence* and *Chickadee*, received the Scott O'Dell Award for Historical Fiction. Erdrich has won numerous awards for her novels, short stories, and poems. Her recent novel for adults, *The Night Watchman* (2020), won the Pulitzer Prize for Fiction, and in 2020 Erdrich received a Lifetime Achievement Award from the Native Writers' Circle of the Americas.

Erdrich holds a bachelor's degree in English from Dartmouth College and a master's degree in Writing from Johns Hopkins University. Erdrich currently lives in Minneapolis.

Kusugak, Michael (Inuit, Canada)

Michael Kusugak is an Inuk writer of works of fiction and nonfiction for children. *The Curse of the Shaman* (2006) is Kusugak's only novel and only written work for readers ages 10 and up. Kusugak has published many books for younger children, most notably *Baseball Bats for Christmas* (1990), *Northern Lights: The Soccer Trails* (1993), *Arctic Stories* (1998), *The Littlest Sled Dog* (2008), *The Most Amazing Bird* (2020), and his first book, *A Promise Is a Promise*, co-written by Robert Munsch.

Kusugak was born in 1948 at a point of land called Qatiktalik (Cape Fullerton) on the west side of Hudson Bay and spent the first part of his life at Repulse Bay, Nunavut. In 1948, Kusugak's parents and grandparents lived traditionally as Inuit people by hunting and fishing, wearing traditional seal and caribou-skin clothes, traveling by dogsled and kayak, and sleeping in igloos and skin tents. All of Kusugak's books, including his only novel, *The Curse of the Shaman* (2006), feature Inuit people living in traditional ways that reflect his own childhood experiences.

Kusugak was forced to attend school, his first residential school, in 1954 at Chesterfield Inlet many miles southward by airplane from his family's home at Repulse Bay. He went on to attend several other residential schools before graduating from high school in Saskatoon and attending university. Kusugak finally pursued a writing career in the late 1980s, at Robert Munsch's suggestion.

In 2008, Kusugak was the recipient of the Vicky Metcalf Award for Literature for Young People, honoring him for his lifetime contribution to Canadian children's literature. Today, Kusugak travels widely from his home near Lake Winnipeg in northern Manitoba, sharing his stories with children.

Maracle, Lee (Sto: loh, Canada)

Lee Maracle (1950–2011) was a member of the Sto: loh Nation, born and raised in North Vancouver, British Columbia. Maracle wrote one novel for adolescent readers, *Will's Garden* (2002), five novels for adults, several collections of short stories and poems, and nonfiction works focusing primarily on the lives of Indigenous women.

In 2009 and 2019 respectively, Maracle received honorary doctorates from St. Thomas University and the University of Waterloo. For varying periods of time, she served as writer in residence (University of Toronto First Nations House, University of Guelph), visiting professor and instructor (University of Waterloo, University of Toronto, Western Washington University), and cultural director for the Indigenous Theatre School in Toronto.

In 2018, for her outstanding contributions to Canadian literature and service to the nation, Maracle was named an officer of the Order of Canada.

Slipperjack, Ruby (Ojibwe, Canada)

Ruby Slipperjack-Farrell is a member of the Eabametoong First Nation in Ontario. She has written six novels for middle grade readers including *Honour the Sun* (1987), *Silent Words* (1992), *Weesquachak and the Lost Ones* (2000), *Little Voice* (2001), *Dog Tracks* (2008), and *These Are My Words* (2016). The majority of these novels focus on contemporary Anishinabe people, their language, and culture. Slipperjack-Farrell speaks the Anishinabe language fluently.

Slipperjack-Farrell was born at Whitewater Lake in Ontario in 1952 and spent the first part of her life on her father's trapline. Between the years of 1988 and 2005, Slipperjack-Farrell earned undergraduate and graduate degrees in history and education.

In 2017, Slipperjack-Farrell received the Vicky Metcalf Award for Literature for Young People, honoring her for her lifetime contribution to Canadian children's literature and retired shortly thereafter from her position as professor of education in the Indigenous Learning Department at Lakehead University in Thunder Bay, Ontario, where she currently resides.

Tingle, Tim (Choctaw, United States)

Tim Tingle is a member of the Choctaw Nation of Oklahoma and has written 20 books for young people and a series of self-published novels for adults (*Travis Lee* Series, Books 1–12). Tingle's novels for younger readers, ages 10–12, include *House of Purple Cedar* (2014), *When a Ghost Talks, Listen* (2018), and *Stone River Crossing* (2019). He has also produced four collections of short stories or tales for this same age group.

For Tingle's first two novels, *House of Purple Cedar* (2014) and *How I Became A Ghost* (2013/2015), he received the American Indian Youth Literature Award in the categories of middle school and young adult readers respectively.

Tingle has also written two series of novels for older readers, ages 12–16, published by 7th Generation Books. The *Danny Blackgoat* series includes *Danny Blackgoat, Navajo Prisoner* (2013), *Danny Blackgoat, Rugged Road to Freedom* (2014), and *Danny Blackgoat, Dangerous Passage* (2017). The *No Name* series includes *No Name* (2014), *No More No Name* (2017), *A Name Earned* (2018), *Trust Your Name* (2018), and *Name Your Mountain* (2020).

Tingle holds bachelor's and master's degrees in English and English literature from the University of Texas and University of Oklahoma respectively. Tingle was a featured speaker at the National Museum of the American Indian in 2006–2007 and is a featured storyteller at special storytelling events throughout the United States.

White, Tara (Mohawk, Canada)

Tara White is a member of the Mohawk Nation from Kahnawake, Quebec. She holds a master's degree in business administration and is a certified management accountant. *Where I Belong* (2014) is White's first novel. White published her first picture book for children, *I Like Who I Am*, in 2016. White currently lives in Bowmanville, Ontario.

METHODOLOGY: THE IDENTIFICATION AND GROUPING OF INDIGENIZING FEATURES

The identification and grouping of indigenizing features for the 24 fictional worlds examined in this book was achieved using the resources of Systemic-Functional Linguistics (Halliday and Matthiessen 2014) and a method of analysis focused on close reading and the identification, classification, cross-classification, coding, recoding, and reclassification of specific linguistic (lexicogrammatical) units that construe the distinctive experiences of Canadian and American Indigenous peoples in real and imaginary worlds.

Systemic-Functional Linguistic Resources

Systemic-Functional Linguistics (SFL) is a theory of language that focuses on the function or functioning of language in social contexts. Systemic-Functional linguists are keenly interested in the workings of language in various social contexts, how language is used for particular purposes, and the choices language users make in their selection of words and wordings to achieve particular purposes. The distinctive resources provided by SFL enable linguists and others to gain valuable insights about the meanings construed by a wide range of texts including novels intended for readers ages 10–16.

Analytic Method

The first novel and fictional world examined for indigenizing features was *The Porcupine Year* (Erdrich 2008). A close reading of this novel yielded a large set of idea units that were marked in the text, then transferred to paper for sorting and grouping. Table 2.1 shows sets of idea units for four chapters in *The Porcupine Year*.

The idea units shown in table 2.1 include one-word nouns in English or Ojibwe (canoe, healer, awl, *asiniig*, *weyass*, *adizookaan*), common Ojibwe expressions (*gawin*), people's names (Omakayas, Light Moving in the Leaves), described nouns (beaded sheath), classified nouns (helping spirit),

Table 2.1. Idea units from four chapters in *The Porcupine Year* (2008)

Chapter	Idea Units
1	Omakayas, canoe, good hunter, *asiniig*, Anishinabe, *miigwech*
2	between a child and a woman, exile, *gaawin*, made canoe, beaded sheath, sinew, set a snare, catch a rabbit, rebraided the sinew loop, Quillboy, warrior, medicine animal, warrior talk, helping spirit, killed a moose or beaver, roasted fish
10	tea brewed from the needles and roots of balsam trees, coat made of furs, adopt the abandoned children, weaving twine, basswood twine, set rabbit snares, fat rabbits, rabbit blanket, highbush cranberries, kill a deer, manoomin, dried *weyass*, pemmican, stored seeds (corn, potato, squash), medicine plants (staghorn sumac, mugwort, milkweed, *oja'cidji'bik* leaves, sweetgrass, sweet flag), medicinal drink, treat bleeding, strengthen heart, heal bruises, cure boils, treat colds, coughs, toothaches, cramps, fevers, reeds used for weaving mats, healer, skin clothes, rabbit fur lining, medicine bag, becoming-young-woman ceremony, birchbark house, balsam tea, mashed cattail roots, banked their birchbark house with earth and leaves
16	sugar maples, sugar camp, tapped the trees, boiled down their own syrup over great fires, tended fires day and night, personal traplines, personal hunting areas, medicine ceremonies, Anishinabeg from southern shores and the Plains, Metis woman, sugar-making time, new carved spoon, new carved wooden bowl, little bear ornamentation, carved paddle, awl, *adizookaan* (sacred story, magical story), recount of a person's life experiences, Light Moving in the Leaves (a person's name), smallpox, burned everything her family owned during sickness, dogsled, sucked bones, carried the weight of life itself, her own strength, spirit bundle, noble old woman, woman lodge, sacred island, becoming-a-woman teachings, lichen and root stew, predicting bad weather, dreams, medicine storage, magical islands, quills

verbs + objects (set a snare, killed a moose or beaver), verbs + objects + additional elements (boiled down their own syrup over great fires, tended fires day and night, banked their birchbark house with earth and leaves), and nouns + embedded clauses (tea brewed from needles and roots of balsam trees).

In most cases, for all 24 novels examined in this book, all the words that appear in an idea unit were found in the same sentence. Occasionally, however, one or more words were drawn from several sentences in the same paragraph or from paragraphs on the same page (e.g., rebraided the sinew loop). Idea units occasionally appear in summative wording, as in warrior talk, which identifies Quillboy's speech in chapter 2 as warrior-like. Occasionally for clarity, an idea unit includes a word inferred from a sentence or paragraph context, as in "stored" seeds and "personal" traplines.

Idea units for *The Porcupine Year* (Erdrich 2008) and six other novels were the focus of the first of four grouping and labeling cycles. The first cycle yielded four primary groupings of indigenizing features, Groups A–D. During the next three cycles, as the initial list of indigenizing features grew from the analysis of fictional worlds in the remaining 17 novels, two of the four Group labels changed, as shown in table 2.2.

Likewise, as shown in table 2.3, more than half of the initial 10 Category labels changed, and two new Categories were added in response to an ever-expanding list of indigenizing features produced from the analysis of additional fictional worlds. (In chapters 3–9 mainly for manageability and enhanced readability, some Categories of indigenizing features are clustered in tertiary groupings called sets.)

Labeling changes during the final grouping and labeling cycle were driven, on one hand, by the author's refined understandings of indigenizing features as the result of a sustained and comprehensive analysis of fictional worlds in 24 Indigenous novels and, on the other hand, by necessary cross-referencing and the adoption of concepts (conceptual labels) preferred by Indigenous scholars and writers.

Four cycles of grouping and labeling also produced a significant number of reworded indigenizing feature labels. Some examples of initial and reworded labels for Groups A–D Categories 1, 4, 5, 8, and 10 are shown in table 2.4.

Table 2.2. Groups A–D label changes after four grouping and labeling cycles

Group	First Grouping and Labeling Cycle	Fourth Grouping and Labeling Cycle
Group A	Time, History, Ancestry	Retained
Group B	Beliefs, Values, Traditions	Cultural Beliefs, Values, Events, Traditions
Group C	Communication, Kinship, Socialization	Language, Storytelling, Family Life, Kinship
Group D	Destruction and Restoration	Retained

Table 2.3. Category revision during four grouping and labeling cycles

First Grouping and Labeling Cycle	Fourth Grouping and Labeling Cycle
1. Time	1. Time
2. Tribal History	2. Tribal History
3. Ancestry	3. Ancestry
4. Religious Beliefs and Practices	4. Religious Beliefs and Practices
5. Nationhood and Community Values	5. Cultural Values
6. Traditions	6. Cultural Events
7. Language Use, Communication, Stories, Storytelling	7. Cultural Traditions
8. Socialization, Teaching, Learning	8. Language Use, Stories, Storytelling
9. Kinship	9. Family Life and Kinship
10. Divestments, Discrimination, Defense, Disease, Leadership	10. Denigration, Subjugation, Disease
11. —	11. Defense and Leadership
12. —	12. Restoration and Recovery

Table 2.4. Initial and reworded labels for individual features in selective categories

Group, Category	Initial Label	Reworded Label
A1 Time	seasonal cycles	seasonal activity cycle seasonal habitation cycles
B4 Religious Beliefs and Practices	spirit protectors	spirit helpers, guides, protectors
B5 Cultural Values	reciprocity and sharing	valuing sharing and peaceful relationship with neighboring nations
C8 Language Use, Stories, Storytelling	folk heroes	stories about culture heroes stories about legendary individuals stories about animal tricksters widely circulated stories of contemporary renown
D10 Divestments, Denigration, Subjugation, Disease	discrimination or racism	cultural denigration disdain harassment subjugation brutality

REFERENCES

Halliday, Michael, and Christian Matthiessen. *Halliday's Introduction to Functional Grammar*. 4th ed. Abingdon, Oxon: Routledge, 2014.

Chapter 3

Group A

Time, History, Ancestry

CHAPTER OVERVIEW

Indigenizing fictional world features in Group A and the Categories of Time, Tribal History, and Ancestry are examined in this chapter. In all, 12 indigenizing features are identified, described, and illustrated in this chapter.

1. Time: seasonal activity cycle, seasonal habitation cycles, prescience, dreamtime
2. Tribal History: notable people, events, places
3. Ancestry: ancestral lands, identity, beings, scents, symbols

1. TIME

Four time-focused features distinguish indigenized fictional worlds. Fictional world events in all three novels in the *Birchbark House* series are organized by seasonal activity cycles largely driven by the availability of food, and events in these and three other novels are framed by and integrally tied to seasonal relocation patterns. Prominent individuals in five novels learn about future events from prescient others that will personally affect them, or participate in a sequence of events that spans both real and imagined worlds.

Seasonal Activity Cycle

Fictional world events in the *Birchbark House* novels unfold sequentially season by season (summer through spring) during the yearly cycle of seasonal activities engaged in by most sovereign Ojibwe people for the period of

1847–1852. Seasonal activity highlights for the first novel in the series, *BH* (1847–1848), follow.

Summer Season Activity Highlights. Tanning hides. Making baskets. Harvesting blueberries. Tending the corn field. Protecting the corn field. Gifting items acquired by trade. Net fishing.

Fall Season Activity Highlights. Drying fish. Repairing fish nets. Weaving new mats for winter use. Tanning hides. Producing new winter clothes. Repairing canoes. Harvesting and drying chokecherries. Repairing the winter cabin. Harvesting and preparing wild rice. Making corn meal. Caching food for the winter. Collecting and preparing medicinal plants. Collecting and preparing acorns. Cooking and eating seasonal meats (beaver). Drying deer meat for the winter.

Winter Season Activity Highlights. Repairing the winter cabin. Sharing sacred stories. Trapping animals. Decorating clothes and containers. Making dance fans. Making new clothes. Ice fishing. Attending special wintertime dances. Snaring rabbits. Cooking and eating seasonal meats (rabbit).

Spring Season Activity Highlights. Building a new birchbark house. Planting corn. Collecting maple sap and making syrup and candies. Bow and arrow making. Gifting items acquired by trade.

Seasonal Habitation Cycles

Prominent individuals in four novels, including Omakayas and her family members in the three *Birchbark House* novels, change residences from one season to the next, travel to each new residence by foot, by canoe, or by dog-sled, and engage in specific traditional activities at the new seasonal location. In *COTS* chapter 11, The-man-with-no-eyebrows leads his family by foot to their summer camp on the northern coast of a small bay (now Rankin Inlet), a place they return to often each year in early spring.

In *BH*, Omakayas and her family spend most of the year, winter to early fall, on an island called the Island of the Golden-Breasted Woodpecker (Moningwanykaning in Ojibwe, now Madeline Island), north of Chequamegon Bay on Lake Superior. The family spends the winter in a cedarwood cabin and spends the spring in a new birchbark house built for them by the oldest member of the household, Nokomis, Omakayas's grandmother. In the fall, the family relocates to their rice camp south of the island on the mainland.

In *GOS* chapter 16, when it is spring, under increasing pressure from the United States government to surrender their lands to European settlers, the family abandons their seasonal habitation cycle on the Island of the Golden-Breasted Woodpecker, leaves the island by canoe, and relocates to the Lake of the Woods many miles northward. The family's long journey is reported in *TPY*.

Prescience (foresight)

The online *American Heritage Dictionary* defines prescience as foresight or one's knowledge of actions or events before they occur.[1] Prominent individuals in two novels learn about future events from a prescient bird or man. In *LLM*, Lana learns about the prescient call of an owl which often forewarns people of the imminent death of a loved one (92). In *WP*, Saxso learns from a local Abenaki man nicknamed The Worrier about the imminent destruction of their village. Saxso identifies the man as a *medawlinnoak*, one who sees beyond the visible world (19–20).

Dreamtime

Prominent individuals in three novels locate a missing loved one, reexperience the past as an ancestor, or defeat a monster in a timeless dreamtime world both real and imaginary. In *GOS* chapter 14, Omakayas travels through the air one night in a dream, arrives at a distant island, and spots her missing father sitting alone by a familiar black rock, recording the passage of time on a counting stick (209). In *WG*, in a dream-like state, neither fully awake nor fully sleeping, Will recalls his ancestral life from over a century ago and snippets of old stories about Raven, eagles, mountains, and trees (5–7).

In *SM*, in a fast-paced dream spanning two chapters, Molly speeds through the forest in the middle of the night hotly pursued by the Skeleton Man. The trail through the forest looks vaguely familiar to Molly, but the river ahead is completely unknown to her and offers no passage across. The Skeleton Man appears to Molly for the first time at the top of a steep hill directly behind her. But in his hasty descent, he loses his footing on the slippery slope, comes crashing down the hill, and lands with a great splash in the river.

But this is not the end of the Skeleton Man, as Molly soon learns. The Skeleton Man hotly pursues her again on her new trail uphill. This new trail takes Molly high up a hill to the head of a great waterfall and a fallen tree that offers Molly safe passage across the river here at its high point on the hill.

At her heels, now crossing the falls himself on the same fallen tree with his hypnotic eyes locked on her, is the Skeleton Man. Molly looks forcefully away, breaks the other's hypnotic hold on her, grasps the end of the fallen tree firmly, and with all her strength casts the tree in the river. Molly's dream ends with the Skeleton Man caught in the river current and tumbling over the falls to his death.

2. TRIBAL HISTORY

Prominent individuals in five novels learn about or recall notable leaders, notable events, or a notable place in their own tribal histories. These individuals identify themselves as Shawnee, Narragansett, Lakota, Abenaki, or Ojibwe. Brief or detailed accounts of specific tribal histories offered by an Indigenous person is a distinguishing feature of indigenized fictional worlds.

Notable People

Prominent individuals in two novels have substantial personal knowledge, gained from conversations with a parent or grandparent, about important Indigenous leaders in early American history and their own tribal histories. In *DP*, during a visit to the local library, Armie recalls biographical details about the Shawnee leader Tecumseh (c. 1768–1813) shared with him by his mother (84–85). In *WITD*, after receiving a prank phone call, Maddy recalls key biographical details about the great Narragansett leader Canonchet (d. 1676) shared with her by her grandmother (9–12).

Notable Events

Prominent individuals in two novels learn about or recall notable events in their tribal histories. In *LLM*, Lana learns from her grandfather about her Lakota ancestors' last buffalo hunt (84–86). In *WP* chapter 2, while standing outside the dance hall on the night that he learns about an imminent attack on his village, Saxso recalls the massacre of his Abenaki ancestors at Turner's Falls in 1676 (14–15).

Notable Places

In *SW*, near Best Island on Whitewater Lake, on his summertime travels by canoe with an old Ojibwe man, Danny, Ojibwe himself, passes an important burial site for Ojibwe people that is all but forgotten by most people now who live in the area (156).

3. ANCESTRY

Ancestral lands, beings, scents, or symbols are identified in 20 novels, and the ancestral identity of prominent individuals and others is identified in all 24 novels. Single or multiple references to Indigenous ancestry is a distinguishing feature of indigenized fictional worlds.

Ancestral Lands

An identification or description of a territory or geographical feature of specific ancestral importance to an Indigenous Nation appears in 14 novels. Geographic features identified or described in one or more of these novels include mountains, canyons, hills, valleys, islands, inlets, points of land, cemeteries, lakes, rivers, falls, and trees.

Ancestral Territories

1. Five Nations territories (*COTL,* front map)
2. Kahnawake (*WIB* 83)

Ancestral Mountains, Canyons, Hills, and Valleys

1. The Black Hills (*LLM* 67)
2. Adirondacks (*DP* 85)
3. Cheam Mountain (*WG* 6–7)
4. Canyon del Chelly (*DBDP* 40)
5. Big Nose hill (*COTL* 104)
6. Mohawk River valley (*COTL* 22)

Ancestral Islands, Inlets, Points of Land, and Cemeteries

1. A well-known sacred island (*TPY* 142)
2. A legendary island called *Odzihozo* (*WP* 153)
3. An island commonly called *Ochichakominising* by the local people (*SW* 142)
4. Various named islands and a point of land including *Salliq* (an island called Farther-out-to-sea), *Uqsuriak* (originally Oil Slick Island, now Marble Island), Big-igloo Island, Soapstone Island, and Dead Man Island (*COTS* 7, 4, 109, 127)
5. *Kangiquliniq* (a small inlet, *COTS* 47)
6. *Siuraarjuk* (Bit-of-sand, a point of land, *COTS* 4) and *Tikirajuaq* (Long-forefinger, a point of land, *COTS* 37)
7. Crown Point (*WP,* front map)
8. A sacred burial ground in Kahnawake (*WIB* 83)
9. An ancient Indigenous burial site commonly known as the Swan Point Cemetery and other burial sites in the region (*WITD* 29–30)

Ancestral Lakes, Rivers, and Falls

1. *Naujatujuq* (Many-seagulls Lake, just south of In-There, *COTS* 101)
2. [G]lassy lake, a lake in the woods only known to Choctaws (*SRC* 294)
3. Various lakes including Petonbowuk (Lake Champlain), Lake Memphremagog, and Lake George (*WP*, front map)
4. Smoothrock and Whitewater Lakes (*SW* 108, 122)
5. *Ska-no'-dar-io* (The Beautiful Lake, *COTL* 7, 38)
6. Providence and Seekonk Rivers (*WITD* 11, 29)
7. Various rivers including *Skan'-neh-ta-de Ga-hun-da* (The River Beyond the Openings), *Ka-hu-ah'-go Ga-hun-da* (the big river), and *Ga-na-wa-ga Ga-hun-da* (The Rapid River) (*COTL* 7, 37, 38, lower- or upper-case in original)
8. Various rivers including Alsigontikuk (St. Francis River), Kwanitiewk (Connecticut River), Winooski River, Lamoille River, Missisquoi River, Yamaska River, White River, and St. Lawrence River (*WP*, front map)
9. Fish River (*COTS* 135)
10. *Ne-ah-gah* (the big falls, *COTL* 38)

Ancestral Trees

1. Sequoia (*WP* 101)
2. Cedar (*GOS* 67, *WP* 7)
3. Tamarack (*LV* 48)
4. Pine (*LV* 48, *GOS* 68)
5. Maple (*TPY* 168)
6. Birch (*GOS* 67)

Ancestral Identity

An ancestral identity is a personal identification that connects a contemporary Indigenous person to a cultural group from the distant past. Ancestral identities may be broad (e.g., Mohawk) or narrow (e.g., Huron). Prominent individuals in all 24 novels identify themselves ancestrally as Anishinabe (Ojibwe), Mohawk, Navajo, Abenaki, Choctaw, Lakota, Sto: loh, Inuit, Shawnee, or Narragansett.

Ancestral identifications for all 24 novels appear in table 3.1. For convenience, these identifications are grouped by the temporal setting of the given fictional world—a setting that is past (historical), present (contemporary), or future (fantasy). Prominent ancestral identifications appear in bold, and multiple ancestral identifications appear in a substantial number of the novels (e.g., *WG* and *MT*, seven identifications each).

Table 3.1. Ancestral identifications in historical, contemporary, and fantasy worlds

Historical worlds

Nation(s)	Novel	Page(s)
Anishinabe (Ojibwe)	*BH, TPY*	1; xi
Abenaki (Anen:tak), **Mohawk** (Flint), Huron, Oneida (Standing Stone), Onondaga (Fire-keepers)	*COTL*	5, 7, 38, 121
Navajo	*DB books*	*NP*: 7; *RRTF*: 1; *DP*: 5.
Lakota (Bwaanag), **Ojibwe** (Anishinabeg)	*GOS*	7, 20
Abenaki, Mohawk, Seneca, Chickahominy	*MTTT*	8, 115, 171, 191
Choctaw	*SRC*	2
Abenaki, Skaticook (cf. Schaghticoke), Mohawk	*WP*	5, 8, 24

Contemporary worlds

Nation(s)	Novel	Page(s)
Indian, Abenaki, Mohican	*HR*	117
Ojibway, Cree	*HTS*	15
Lakota, Cheyenne	*LLM*	7, 36
Ojibwa, Mohawk	*LV*	7, 113
Choctaw, Cherokee	*NN books*	8, 108; 2, 28
Ojibwa	*SW*	41
Northern Salish, Tsimshians, Squamish, **Sto: loh**, Cree, Iroquois	*WG*	48, 80, 89, 190
Mohawk	*WIB*	49

Fantasy worlds

Nation(s)	Novel	Page(s)
Inuit, Unaliit, Iqqiliit	*COTS*	2, 76
Shawnee	*DP*	5
Cree, Metis, **Anishnaabe**, Inuit, Haudenosaunee, Migmaw, Ho-Chunk	*MT*	20, 21, 23, 144, 169
Mohawk	*SM*	3
Narragansett	*WITD*	xi

Ancestral Beings

Ancestral beings are supernatural beings known to members of an Indigenous Nation in the distant past. Ancestral beings are identified by prominent individuals in 14 novels. These beings, shown in table 3.2, appear in a traditional story, personal recollection, or personal recount; and they range from celestial beings and birds to monsters and subterranean little people.

Table 3.2. Ancestral beings identified in 14 novels

Being	Novel	Page(s)	Nation
elder brother the Sun	COTL	119	Mohawk
forest dwellers	WP	23, 88	Abenaki
Grandma moon	WG	117	Sto: loh
little people	GOS, TPY, LV, SW, COTL, WP	103–110; 21, 33; 7; 97; 23, 29; 46	Ojibwe, Mohawk, Abenaki
man in the lake	NN	69	Choctaw
monsters	WITD, DP	16, 24; 105	Narragansett, Shawnee
raven	WG	6	Sto: loh
skeleton man monster	SM	3	Mohawk
sky beings	COTL	26	Mohawk
spirit people	SRC	252	Choctaw
spirits	LV, BH	94, 101	Ojibwe
stars	DP	90	Shawnee
thunder beings	COTL, MTTT, GOS	39; 5, 282; 89	Mohawk, Abenaki, Ojibwe
windigo	BH	13, 101, 171	Ojibwe

Ancestral Monsters in *DP*

Six different types of ancestral water monsters are identified in *DP* (86). These monsters are simply identified or briefly described by Armie, who encounters them in various collections of Abenaki and Iroquois stories on reserve at his school library. The six types of monsters include giant beavers, giant fish, sucking monsters and huge horned serpents that live in the ocean and lakes, strange hairy creatures that hide in natural springs, and Toad woman.

Ancestral Little People in Six Novels

Ancestral little people are identified in six novels and appear in a traditional story or personal account shared by a prominent Ojibwe, Mohawk, or Abenaki individual. Little (stone-throwing) people (*Iakotinenioia'ks* in Mohawk) appear in a mythical story recalled by Otsi:stia in *COTL* (23). Basic details about little people (*Memegwesiwag* in Ojibwe) are recalled by Ray in *LV* (7) and reported by Ol' Jim in *SW* (97). Detailed personal encounters with individual little people (*memegwesi* in Ojibwe) are recounted by Omakayas in *TPY* (21, 33) and Nokomis in *GOS* (103–10).

In *COTL*, while filling their baskets with fresh strawberries one morning, Herons Flying tells her daughter Otsi:stia about the helpfulness of little people in their lives. Otsi:stia learns from her mother that the village crops

were watered faithfully each night with dew carried by little people in minia-
ture cups, and that little people guarded the entrance of caves near the village
and stopped the monsters that lived deep underground from emerging and
hurting people.

In *GOS* chapter 7, in late autumn, Omakayas's grandmother Nokomis
recounts two life-saving encounters with the same *memegwesi*, one little man,
when she was eight years old (103–10). The same little man appeared to her
twice in the woods, once in the summer and once in the winter. In her first
encounter with the little man, she was lost, and he comforted her until her
grandparents had found her. In her second encounter with the little man, she
and her grandparents were desperately hungry, and he helped her to find food,
a sleeping bear beneath the snow.

Ancestral Scents

Specific aromatic scents produced from natural materials commonly harvested by members of an Indigenous Nation in the distant past continue to be
used for ceremonial and other purposes by contemporary Indigenous peoples.
Ancestral scents including the aromatic scent of cedar, tobacco, pine, and
sweetgrass are identified by prominent individuals in five novels.

1. *Cedar scent. SRC.* Southeastern United States. "[Shonti] passed a burning bundle of cedar over Lil Mo's head, circling the room, smoking the
   house with the sweet and cleansing smell of cedar" (213).
2. *Cedar scent. HR.* Northeastern United States. "There seemed to be as
   much said by Uncle Louis's silence as there were in the words others spoke. It was comfortable—comfortable as the smell of cedar and
   smoke that was as much a part of him as that green guide's hat or his
   moccasins" (33).
3. *Cedar scent. BH.* Northeastern United States. "As it grew dark, the
   family ate makuks of moose stew and fresh greens and berries, licked
   their fingers and bowls clean, and at last rolled themselves into warm
   fluffy rabbit-skin blankets that still smelled of the cedary smoke of their
   winter cabin" (12).
4. *Tobacco scent. BH.* Northeastern United States. "At the base of the tree,
   Nokomis left her offering [of tobacco], sweet and fragrant" (8).
5. *Cedar and tobacco scents. MT.* Central Canada. "Tobacco. Cedar. And
   the thick curl of something more, something I thought I'd only ever
   smelled with the memory of smell" (168).
6. *Pine scent. HTS.* Central Canada. "I can smell the fresh moist spring air
   and the pine scent when I pass the stand of pine trees" (181).

7. *Sweetgrass scent*. *MT*. Central Canada. "[Francis] was right in front of me now, her face an inch from mine. She smelled like sweetgrass and a deeper smoke" (180).

Ancestral Symbols

The online *Oxford English Dictionary* defines a symbol as something that stands for, represents, or denotes something else (not by exact resemblance, but by vague suggestion, or by some accidental or conventional relation); especially a material object representing or taken to represent something immaterial or abstract, as a being, idea, quality, or condition; a representative or typical figure, sign, or token; occasionally a type (of some quality).[2]

Ancestral symbols are identified by prominent individuals in six novels. These symbols are ancestral to Lakota, Choctaw, Sto: loh, Mohawk, Navajo, and Abenaki people and include the morning star (*LLM* 30), the diamond shape (*SRC* 83), family crests (*WG* 23), wampum (*COTL* 87), and circles (*DBRRTF* 94, *WP* 159).

The Morning Star

In *LLM*, while cutting diamond shapes for a new star quilt, Lori asks her grandmother why she always makes these particular types of quilts. Her grandmother tells her that the first Lakota women living on reservations made quilts from the leftover pieces of cloth from their new reservation clothes and modeled a quilt after the inspirational Morning Star, a symbol of newness—a new day and new beginning. And thus was born a new tradition, reported her grandmother.

The Diamond Shape

In *SRC* chapter 16, "Funi Man the Teacher," Funi Man teaches Lil Mo about the Choctaw people who live on this side of the river opposite the plantation from which Lil Mo recently escaped. Funi Man's teachings focus on many topics, including unusual Choctaw people like Shonti, a medicine woman who owns six rattlesnakes. Lil Mo learns from Funi Man that Choctaw people wear diamond shapes on their clothes similar to the diamond shape that appears on a rattlesnake's back—to honor rattlesnakes, a sacred animal for Choctaw people (82–83).

Family Crests

In *WG*, Will identifies his father as a commercial carver who specially adorns many of his carved bowls, spoons, and plates with family crests (23). As noted in the online *Canadian Encyclopedia*, crests are a type of heraldic art that often adorn objects given as gifts during potlatch ceremonies.[3] A crest often contains the image of an animal, real or imagined, but the crest's meaning typically transcends any particular association with an animal. A carved object adorned with a family crest reminds its owner of the mythic past.

Wampum

In *COTL* Part 2, chapter 7, Otsi:stia attends an important meeting one night at the big longhouse in her village. Inside the longhouse, Otsi:stia spots her eldest uncle Big Tree with the wampum draped across his palm. All important meetings begin this way in her village, with the wampum displayed by its official keeper, her uncle Big Tree.

Events in *COTL* take place in the late 1400s. At this point in time, the wampum served three important ceremonial purposes for Mohawk people, and these three purposes appear in Otsi:stia's thoughts when she sees the wampum in her uncle's hand and admires its design and meaning. The design of the wampum is simple but thoughtful. Special spiral shells are strung together with thread and mounted securely on a strip of deer hide. In the late 1400s, the wampum carried important messages, helped people to remember agreements, and explained relationships between different nations (87).

One Circle

In *DBRRTF* chapter 13, Danny Blackgoat's grandfather seeks to cleanse Danny of his recent experiences with death by positioning him at the center of a circle formed by family members (94). This Navajo purification practice is described later in this book in the section "Purification Practices" in chapter 4.

Concentric Circles

In *WG* chapter 29, Saxso notes the passage of time and renewal of his village. Some months have passed since his return to St. Francis with his mother and sisters, and Saxso is grateful for the new houses that sprang up from the charred remains of the old village. In a private conversation with the Worrier one morning, Saxso reflects on the return of his loved ones and restoration of his village and notes the circular pattern of people's lives. The Worrier responds by tracing a circle in the sand, then drawing another circle within it.

For the Worrier, a fictional Abenaki visionary, the inner circle represents Abenaki people, and the outer circle represents the Creator. He tells Saxso that all Abenaki people are connected to each other and the Creator; and that is the meaning of the concentric circles he draws in the sand.

NOTES

1. *American Heritage Dictionary*, s.v. "prescience (n.)," accessed February 4, 2023, https://www.ahdictionary.com/prescience.

2. *Oxford English Dictionary*, s.v. "symbol (n.)," accessed February 4, 2023, https://www.oed.com/symbol.

3. *Canadian Encyclopedia*, entry *crests* in article "Northwest Coast Indigenous Art," accessed February 4, 2023, https://www.thecanadianencyclopedia.ca/northwest-coast-aboriginal-art.

Chapter 4

Group B

Cultural (Religious) Beliefs

CHAPTER OVERVIEW

Indigenizing fictional world features in Group B and the Category of Religious Beliefs and Practices are examined in this chapter. Two sets of Category 4 features are examined. In all, 15 indigenizing features are identified, described, and illustrated in this chapter.

4. Religious Beliefs and Practices
    4.1: Central religious beliefs: beliefs about the Creator, cosmic coherence, spirit helpers, guides, protectors; spiritual travel, supernatural powers, visions
    4.2: Sacred religious practices and objects: praying and prayers, sacred offerings, sacred songs, medicine bags, spirit bundles, sacred objects, sacred drums and drumming, honoring the dead, purification practices

4. RELIGIOUS BELIEFS AND PRACTICES

Central religious beliefs and sacred religious practices and objects are identified and described in varying detail by prominent individuals in 18 novels. Central religious beliefs focus on the Creator of specific Indigenous nations, cosmic coherence, spiritual travel, supernatural powers, the personal and collective importance of visions, the importance of sacred offerings, prayers, and songs; and the key role played by spirit helpers, guides, or protectors. Sacred religious beliefs, practices, and objects are all distinguishing features of indigenized fictional worlds.

SET 4.1 CENTRAL RELIGIOUS BELIEFS

Beliefs About the Creator

Pioneer ethnologists like Lewis Henry Morgan (1818–1881), who lived in North American Indigenous communities for substantial periods of time during the 19th and early 20th centuries and learned firsthand about the people's spiritual beliefs, reported the shared belief among North American Indigenous communities in a Supreme Being or Deity, commonly referred to in English as the Creator.

As in the online *American Heritage Dictionary*, the proper nouns Creator and God are often used synonymously.[1] But many North American Indigenous peoples, past and present, use(d) the words Creator and *Great Spirit* synonymously, although specific names for the Creator appear in many Indigenous languages.

Historical and contemporary beliefs about the Creator are shared in six novels by members of the Mohawk, Ojibwe, and Abenaki Nations. These beliefs are discussed below in terms of collocated meanings: the Creator's dwelling place, qualities, identity, purpose, and guises; traditional ways of addressing and expressing gratitude to the Creator; and seminal communications from the Creator.

Collocations

When thinking or speaking about the Creator alone or with others, prominent fictional world individuals in *COTL*, *GOS*, *TPY*, *WIB*, *WP*, and *LV* use one of eight words, shown below, in the same sentence as the word Creator.

1. Give
2. Keeps safe
3. Pray (to)
4. Bless (with)
5. Bring (home)
6. Take (away)
7. Qualities
8. Disguise

The Creator's Dwelling Place

The Creator dwells in the sky (*COTL* 24, Mohawk).

The Creator's Qualities

The Creator's qualities include greatness and kindness (*WP* 63, Abenaki; *GOS* 236, *TPY* 21, Ojibwe).

The Creator's Identity As Protector, Giver, and Restorer

The Creator is identified as a protector (*TPY* 21, Ojibwe); the giver of blessings and healing knowledge (*COTL* 24, 57, Mohawk), the giver of skills (*TPY* 153, Ojibwe), the giver of voices (*LV* 88, Ojibwe), and the giver of bodily infusions (*WP* 63, Abenaki); the restorer of people's belonging (*WIB* 60, Mohawk) and the balancer of losses and gains (*COTL* 49, Mohawk).

The Creator's Creative Purpose and Guises

In *COTL* chapters 4 and 5, Ohkwa'ri and his twin sister Otsi:stia learn about and ponder the Creator's purpose for Mohawk people and the guises taken by the Creator at different points in time to teach their Clan Mother about the healing properties of plants. In chapter 4, Ohkwa'ri's grandmother teaches him about the Creator's purpose for him and all Mohawk people. Ohkwa'ri learns that the Creator gave them two eyes but only one mouth so Mohawk people would look twice as often as they talked and avoid running into things (50).

In chapter 5, Otsi:stia is reminded of a story about the Creator when she spots a patch of bloodroot flowers blooming at the edge of the strawberry fields. Long ago in the distant past, the Creator visited her clan in the guise of a weak old man who needed to be cared for. The Bear Clan Mother responded kindly to the old man, brought him inside, and cared for him. Illness after illness took hold of him, but each time his body grew weak from a new illness, he shared his knowledge about healing plants with his caregiver, giving her great knowledge about plants, which she passed on to future generations (56–57).

Expressing Gratitude to Gizhe Manidoo

In *GOS*, as Omakayas gets ready to leave her home and homeland as ordered by the United States government, she sits by her brother Neewo's grave and expresses her gratitude to the Gizhe Manidoo, the Creator of all Ojibwe people, for the things provided by the Creator for her and her family (236).

Addressing Skonkwaiatison

In *COTL*, Big Tree addresses the Creator of the Mohawk people, Skonkwaiatison, when everyone in his village gathers by the fields of ripening strawberries to show their gratitude for the bountiful harvest this year (24). He begins his address by calling the Creator's name and identifying the Creator's dwelling place in the sky. He restates the Creator's purpose for creating people, the purpose of their movements on Earth, their need to gather peacefully as a village, and their need to be grateful for ceremonial gatherings such as this.

The main focus of Big Tree's address today is the ripening fruit in the fields. Big Tree reminds his fellow villagers that strawberries and other hanging fruits are seasonal gifts from their Creator, who expects them to congregate, taste each new crop of fruit together, and show their gratitude for these special gifts provided by him.

Skonkwaiatison's Original Instructions

In *COTL* chapter 3, Big Tree recounts the Creator's original instructions to the Mohawk people while sharing a special story with Ohkwa'ri and Otsi:stia one evening in his longhouse (37). The Creator's instructions were easily understood and followed, said Big Tree. Simply stated, Mohawk people everywhere needed to thank their Creator each morning for his gifts of the Earth, all the plants and animals on Earth, and the beings in the sky including the Thunder Beings, Sun, Moon, and Stars.

Cosmic Coherence

Abenaki, Lakota, and many Indigenous peoples, past and present, believe(d) in the existence of a coherent universe, a universe that is systematic, purposeful, and unified. Many contemporary Indigenous peoples believe that their personal being both physical and metaphysical has an orderly and meaningful shape. Prominent individuals in two novels describe their cultural belief in cosmic coherence in terms of directional points.

In *MTTT*, Louis identifies four sacred directions that reflect the coherent ordering of the universe for Abenaki people. Louis learned from his parents that a distinctive land lies in each direction: a dawn land, summer land, sunset land, and winter land (25). In *LLM*, Lori's grandmother distinguishes each cardinal direction by a different color: East (yellow), South (red), North (white), and West (black) (45).

One day after school, Lori joins her grandmother, sister, friend Shoua, and Shoua's mother in her grandmother's living room and listens as her grandmother shares her knowledge about each sacred direction in the Lakota worldview. Later that day, Lori relocates to her room and writes a poem about the four directions.

Cosmic Coherence in Lakota Culture: Four Sacred Directions

According to Lori's grandmother, each sacred direction has its own distinctive set of cultural associations and meanings. East (yellow) is associated with the new day, new life, springtime, and children who will learn about and preserve traditional Lakota culture. South (red) is associated with warmth, midday, summertime, and adults who are now in the prime of their lives and living life fully according to Lakota traditions.

North (white) is associated with snow, evening, wintertime, old age, the hardships endured by elders throughout their long lives, and the wisdom, strength, and courage gained from living through challenging times. West (black) is associated with nighttime, darkness, autumn, and the death of plants, animals, and people.

Spirit Helpers, Guides, Protectors

Spirit guides, helpers, and protectors are identified in *WIB* (95), *BH* (222–26), *TPY* (14–17, 37, 129, 135), *GOS* (194), and *SRC* (80). These guides, helpers, and protectors are embodied in living animals (birds, mammals), deceased relatives, rocks, and stones and are specifically identified as guides, helpers, or protectors.

The crow and baby porcupine are identified as spirit helpers in *BH* (222–26) and *TPY* (14–17, 135) respectively; and respectively in *WIB* (95) and *TPY* (5), the white eagle and river rocks are identified as spirit guides. Spirit protectors are identified in three novels: panther spirit protectors are identified in *SRC* (80); and bear spirit protectors, a deceased relative protector, and spirit protector stones are identified in *TPY* (37, 129) and *GOS* (60, 194).

Spiritual Travel

Prominent individuals in two novels have brief personal encounters with a traveling spirit that seeks them out to warn or comfort them. In *WP*, Saxso has a brief encounter with his friend Samadagwis (57–61), and in *DBNP*, Danny Blackgoat has a brief encounter with his grandfather (129–37).

Spiritual Travel in WP

While relieving himself by the hall, having drank too much cider at the dance taking place inside, Saxso has an unexpected encounter with his friend Samadagwis, who appears to him in a spiritual form and warns him about an imminent danger facing the village (5–9). Samadagwis's spirit has no definitive physical shape but speaks to Saxso audibly and urgently, warning him that the village is surrounded by soldiers who plan to destroy the village and slaughter all of the villagers tonight.

Later that night, while searching frantically among the charred and smoky ruins of his village for his loved ones, Saxso comes upon the very man whose spirit warned him earlier about the impending attack. Now fully back in a bodily form, Samadagwis lies dying in the grass, fatally wounded from the attack that destroyed the village, four bullet holes in his back.

Spiritual Travel in DBNP

Danny Blackgoat's grandfather appears to him in a spiritual form at a frightening moment in Danny's life. At Fort Davis one night, endeavoring to escape his captors, Danny makes his way to the carpentry shop and takes temporary cover in a newly-made coffin. Unexpectedly, the coffin is collected from the carpentry shop the next day by soldiers, transported to the graveyard, sealed, and buried with Danny in it.

Danny manages to stay calm for about an hour, buried underground, then panics, hugs himself tightly, and cries. A moment later, the spirit of his grandfather comes to him, speaks to him consolingly, then appears to him briefly in a visual form, smiling at him. His grandfather's spirit comforts him. Danny takes a deep breath and relaxes.

Supernatural Powers

In *COTS* chapter 3, a man named Paaliaq, who lives with his wife, newborn baby, and elderly mother, is identified as an *angakkuq* (10). The term *angakkuq* was used by Inuit people in the past not only to identify an Inuit man as kinfolk—that is, as the mother's brother (Thalbitzer 1928: 423)—but also to identify an individual as an Inuit shaman. Traditional Inuit shamans like Paaliaq acquired power from the spirit world and used this power to expose wrongdoing against others, expel evil spirits from people and places, cure sicknesses, procure game, and effect changes in the weather (Oosten 1986: 119–20).

Paaliaq's supernatural powers as a shaman are fueled by a largely malevolent spirit that commands the body of a local animal, an arctic ground squirrel, or *siksik* as it is called in Inuktitut in chapters 5 and 7 (26, 29). This spirit or *tuurnngaq* possesses greater supernatural powers than the shaman himself and fulfills the curse issued by Paaliaq in chapter 5 against the newborn son of his friend The-man-with-no-eyebrows.

In chapter 7, The-man-with-no-eyebrows spots Paaliaq's *tuurnngaq* lurking outside and ruminates about the existence of *tuurnngaqs* and their relationship with shamans (30). In The-man-with-no-eyebrow's fictional world, most *tuurnngaqs* commanded the body of a local burrowing animal: a ground squirrel, weasel, or lemming. *Tuurnngaqs* like Paaliaq's possessed powerful magic that they used to fulfill a shaman's curse or spell; and when an old *tuurnngaq* died, the shaman recruited a new one to replace it.

By chapter 15, the midway point in the novel, many years have passed since Paaliaq issued his curse against his friend's son, and his *tuurnngaq* has aged but not yet reached the end of his life. In old age, the *siksik* now recalls his first year of life and the circumstances that brought him and Paaliaq together (94–100). In chapter 15, the aging *siksik* is appropriately referred to as Old Mr. *Siksik* and retains this name until his death in chapter 21.

In chapter 15, Old Mr. *Siksik* recalls the first year of his life, from springtime to autumn, as a relatively normal life for a ground squirrel, happy and free-spirited. But with the arrival of colder weather and his first winter, a dark pall descended on him—a powerful shaman had recruited him as a *tuurnngaq*—and from that point onward, the *siksik*'s life had been very hard and unhappy.

Throughout his long life as Paaliaq's *tuurnngaq*, Old Mr. *Siksik* has followed Paaliaq faithfully in his seasonal travels up and down the coast and has always been ready to use his supernatural powers at Paaliaq's bidding. Ground squirrels are physically equipped for burrowing, but their small bodies, short legs, and delicate feet make long distance travel grueling; and the many journeys Mr. *Siksik* has been forced to undertake through the years with Paaliaq have taken an irreversible physical toll on him.

Old Mr. *Siksik*'s reflections about his life midway through the novel are filled with dread, resentment, and regret. His thoughts are filled with dread about the future and the unknown number of days remaining in his life. He resents his master's mistreatment and neglect of him through the years and the many dangers he has had to face on his own because of his master and mean-spirited others. He resents being called upon by Paaliaq to help people, and regrets that he cannot use his supernatural powers independently.

Visions

The online *American Heritage Dictionary* defines vision as the mystical experience of seeing something that is not in fact present to the eye or is supernatural.[2] In *GOS*, a sequence of future events appears to Omakayas in a vision while she spends time on her own fasting and communicating with the spirits (231–32).

Omakayas's Vision

A five-part vision appears to Omakayas on her third day of fasting in chapter 15. In the first part of the vision, Omakayas sees herself, her parents, and siblings embarking by boat with all of their possessions, and traveling for many days in their crowded family canoe until they finally reach their destination: a beautiful lake with hundreds of islands which appear to Omakayas as spirits, all welcoming her.

In the second and third parts of the vision, Omakayas now sees herself traveling on land in the company of a tall man whose identity is withheld from her. She is older now—her brothers are fully grown and her parents are old—and the world that envelops her now differs sharply from the world of her childhood. With an unknown man beside her, she travels through vast stretches of grass by foot and notes the vastness of the sky and mountainous clouds overhead.

In the fourth part of the vision, a log cabin, a team of horses, ten children, and an old woman all appear to Omakayas in quick succession, children that resemble her and her brothers, and an old woman that turns out to be her. In old age, Omakayas is blind so the children help to seat her comfortably outside, then sit with her and listen attentively to her stories about a childhood pet crow named Andeg.

In the fifth part of the vision, a rapid succession of scenes from the old woman's life appears to Omakayas and leaves her with mixed feelings of joy and sorrow.

SET 4.2 SACRED RELIGIOUS PRACTICES AND OBJECTS

Praying and Prayers

Prominent individuals in all three Danny Blackgoat novels, *NN*, *HR*, *COTL*, *BH*, *TPY*, *GOS*, *WG*, and *LV* pray thankfully to the Creator or seek spiritual strength for themselves or others directly from the Creator or indirectly through an ancestral being (e.g., Salmon Woman, Grandma moon, the sky spirit, an old spirit), an animal spirit (e.g., a deer's spirit), a deceased relative now in spirit form, or a physical manifestation of the Creator (e.g., water, the lighted canyon, streaming sunlight).

Prominent individuals in these 11 fictional worlds pray directly or indirectly to the Creator for courage, reassurance, safe passage, a safe return, restored order, food, prosperity, calmness, healing, a new building, forgiveness, or renewal.

In all three *Danny Blackgoat* novels, Danny Blackgoat repeatedly prays to the Creator for security, calmness, and courage, and thanks the Creator for protecting him and his people before, during, and after their imprisonment by United States soldiers. Danny repeats the same prayer twice in each novel and acknowledges the Creator's unchanging presence in the natural world and within him. He learned the prayer from his grandfather.

Sacred Offerings

Sacred gifts of corn pollen, dry tobacco, or lighted tobacco are offered to the Creator, a physical manifestation of the Creator (a patch of ground in the woods, the lake, the lakeshore), an ancestral being, or a spirit by older and younger members of the Navajo, Mohawk, Sto: loh, and Ojibwe Nations in the three *Danny Blackgoat* novels (3, 140; 67, 96; 7, 157), *WIB* (72), *WG* (9–10), *BH* (7, 183, 202), *TPY* (28), *GOS* (84, 87, 101), *LV* (38), and *SW* (98, 109, 172).

Sacred gifts of corn pollen and dry tobacco are typically stored in special leather pouches. Offerings of corn pollen and tobacco are made in conservative amounts (typically measured in pinches), are given in gratitude, or accompany a prayer for protection, appeasement, renewal, a safe crossing, or a special request.

Sacred Songs

In *LLM*, sacred songs are identified twice. Lori's grandpa recalls a sacred song sung to a dead bison bull during their people's last bison hunt. The song praised the bison for his strength and conveyed the hunters' gratitude to the bison for his life (85). Then at Christmastime, the sound of sacred pow-wow songs fills the living room at Lori's house (109). In *TPY*, in midwinter, Deydey sings a spirit song, seeking courage for himself and his family members and an end to their hunger (111).

Sacred Objects

Sacred objects are identified by prominent individuals in seven novels. These objects include peace pipes (*WIB* 108), medicine bags (*BH* 164, 212–13; *TPY* 107), spirit bundles (*TPY* 121, 179), chant sticks (*SRC* 198, 294), crow and eagle feathers (*WG* 122; *TPY* 51), stones and eagle claws (*WG* 122), and a Cree Bible (*HTS* 15).

Medicine Bags

In *BH* and *TPY*, medicine bags are kept by Omakayas's father Deydey and her grandmother Nokomis. For many North American Indigenous peoples, medicine bags are important personal possessions. A medicine bag is a small leather pouch containing objects such as plant leaves, feathers, shells, rock crystals, or carvings used by their owners for healing purposes (Hirschfelder and Molin 2001). A medicine bag may be owned by a respected family member like Deydey or Nokomis or by a medicine man or woman who conceal the bag in their clothing or suspend it from a cord around their neck or waist.

Spirit Bundles

A spirit bundle is a collection of sacred objects used for healing, protection, good fortune, individual or group empowerment, clairvoyance, or spiritual communication. Spirit bundles may be owned by one or more members of a cultural group, and each object within a bundle is typically connected to a cultural event, belief, ritual, story, song, responsibility, or taboo (Hirschfelder and Molin 2001).

Spirit bundles typically include multiple objects, but the spirit bundle made by Nokomis for Omakayas in *TPY* simply consists of a lock of Old Tallow's hair wrapped in bear fur (121). Omakayas uses her spirit bundle for the purpose of bereavement and offers it food and water for a year (121).

Sacred Drums and Drumming

Drums, identified in *WIB* and *WG* and five other novels, are sacred objects too. Sacred drums, sacred drumming, and hand drum production are identified by prominent individuals in *WIB* (95), *WG* (35), *WP* (18, 33, 35), *NN* (21), *MT* (189), *LLM* (81), and *BH* (208). In *WIB*, Carrie's grandmother explains the purpose and importance of Mohawk drums and drumming. "Drumming is very important to us," says her grandmother. "It's a form of prayer, a form of celebration, an acknowledgment of our ancestors and the good things the Creator has given us" (95).

Honoring the Dead

Prominent individuals in two novels honor the death of a loved one. In *TPY*, Omakayas honors a now late member of her kin group, Old Tallow, on a small island close to home (180). She takes Old Tallow's spirit bundle with her to the island, fasts there alone, and communes with Old Tallow's spirit.

In *LLM*, Lana's family members, friends, and members of her community prepare her body for burial (113–14). Lana's wake service is held the night before the funeral at St. Matthew's church hall. The hall is filled to capacity with people who loved Lana: her family members, her friend Shoua and her parents, her teachers, and students from her school.

Lana's best friend Shoua and her parents approach Lana's grandmother at the service, return a quilt gifted to Shoua some months ago by Lana, and request that the quilt be used to cover Lana as a means of honoring her for her life and friendship. When the service is underway, Shoua rises from her seat and honors her late friend in a short speech with tears coursing down her face. She shares publicly several private memories about Lana and identifies Lana as her sister.

Other people honor Lana in short speeches at her wake service that night. Her classmates speak about her cultural pride and personal strength, how proud she was of her Lakota heritage, and how she defended one of them when he was picked on. Two of Lana's teachers honor her with brief statements, and Father Jim speaks at length about Lana at the start of the service. Father Jim distinguishes Lana as the first girl acolyte at the church, and an excellent acolyte, with her own special gifts.

Purification Practices

Prominent individuals in four novels are spiritually cleansed or purified by wild sage, a cleansing family circle, traditional music, or a sweat lodge. In *WIB*, Carrie learns about the traditional Mohawk practice of self-purification. Her grandmother teaches her to remove bad energy from her life both within and beyond her body by burning wild sage, kneeling on the floor, chanting, and letting the fragrant smoke cleanse her (73).

In *DBRRTF*, members of the Blackgoat family escape to the hills, huddle together in the coming darkness, and form a circle around Danny Blackgoat to cleanse him from his recent encounters with death (94–95). At his grandfather's urging, Danny promptly lowers himself to the ground, sits in a small circle etched for him in the sandy soil, rests his chin on his chest, and shuts his eyes. Danny's grandfather circles the group all night, shaking his rattle gently, and singing a special chant increasingly softly that will remove all traces of evil that for the Navajo accompanies Death.

In *TPY*, Omakayas seeks purification in a newly-built sweat lodge in the presence of all female members of her household—her sister, mother, grandmother, and Old Tallow—as she prepares to receive a new name (54–57). Fragrant plants are placed on heated stones in the sweat lodge, and the doorway is covered to keep the sunlight out. Water is splashed on the heated stones, and soon Omakayas is surrounded by hot steam that burns her wounded face and makes her slightly dizzy.

In *GOS* a year earlier, Omakayas specially invites her friend Break-Apart Girl, an amiable young white girl who attends the same school as Omakayas, to participate in a family purification ceremony (136–41). In this earlier purification ceremony, fragrant tobacco leaves are deposited on the heated stones inside the family sweat lodge, and all the same female members of the household who will come together to purify themselves again a year from now breathe in the streaming hot steam from the stones and fill the dark interior of the sweat lodge with songs and prayers.

NOTES

1. *American Heritage Dictionary*, s.v. "creator (n.)," accessed February 4, 2023, https://www.ahdictionary.com/creator.

2. *American Heritage Dictionary*, s.v. "vision (n.)," accessed February 4, 2023, https://www.ahdictionary.com/vision.

REFERENCES

Hirschfelder, Arlene, and Paulette Molin. *Encyclopedia of Native American Religions.* New York: Checkmark Books, 2001.

Oosten, Jaarich G. "Male and Female in Inuit Shamanism," *Études Inuit Studies* 10, No. 1/2 (1986): 119–20.

Thalbitzer, William. "Die Kültischen Gottheiten der Eskimos," *Archiv für Religionswissenschaft* XXVI, Heft 3/4 (1928): 423.

Chapter 5

Group B

Cultural Values and Events

CHAPTER OVERVIEW

Indigenizing fictional world features in Group B and the Categories of Cultural Values and Events are examined in this chapter. One set of Category 5 features and four sets of Category 6 features are examined. In all, 26 indigenizing features are identified, described, and illustrated in this chapter.

5. Cultural Values: expressing gratitude, valuing dreams, valuing sharing and peaceful relations with neighboring nations; acting calmly, humbly, and honorably; respecting others
6. Cultural Events
   6.1 Traditional games, dancing, and songs: toss and catch, stick and ball games, snow snakes, game of silence; jingle dancers, harvest thunder and moon dances; hoop dance, grass dance, fancy dance, winter gathering dance; traditional songs and singing
   6.2 Family-based feasts: special celebratory event feasts, naming feasts
   6.3 Festivals and special community events: Strawberry Festival, Maple Festival, and Corn Harvest; Spring Festival, Celebratory Dance
   6.4 Ceremonies: Lakota naming ceremony, Choctaw wedding ceremony, Inuit wedding ceremony, Sto: loh becoming man ceremony

5. CULTURAL VALUES

The identification of important cultural values focusing on generosity, calmness, humility, honor, respect, gratitude, peaceful relations with other Indigenous peoples, and dreaming are distinguishing features of indigenized fictional worlds. Prominent individuals in 13 novels identify one or more of these cultural values.

Expressing Gratitude

A prominent individual in four novels identifies the cultural value of gratitude for Choctaw, Mohawk, Shawnee, or Ojibwe people and expresses gratitude to the Creator or a physical manifestation of the Creator for food (*NN* 135, *COTL* 24), the new day (*HR* 63, *LV* 88), a life-supporting and bountiful environment (*COTL* 37), the return of a loved one (*NN* 103), or longevity (*COTL* 116).

In *COTL* chapter 7, Ohkwa'ri and Otsi:stia's uncle Big Tree, a well-respected member of their village and the keeper of the wampum, starts an important Council meeting in the big longhouse by delivering the Thanksgiving Address (88–89). In this address, Big Tree first expresses gratitude to the Creator and the Mother Earth for everyone's life and well-being. Then he thanks the living waters of the earth, the birds, the animals, the life-giving sister plants of corn, bean, and squash, the Thunder Beings, and the invisible messenger beings of the Creator who live in the four directions. Big Tree ends the Thanksgiving Address by thanking the sun, moon, and stars.

Valuing Dreams

A prominent individual in seven novels identifies the value of dreaming for Mohawk, Navajo, Choctaw, and Ojibwe peoples. The online *American Heritage Dictionary* defines a dream as a series of images, ideas, emotions, and sensations occurring involuntarily in the mind during certain stages of sleep.[1] In *WIB*, Carrie values her dreams so greatly that she records them in a special journal (26–28), and the potency of dreams are acknowledged by her grandmother (95). In *SM*, Molly trusts her dreams, as all Mohawk people are taught to trust their dreams (47).

The instructive value of dreams is identified by prominent individuals in five novels. For Navajo, Choctaw, Mohawk, and Ojibwe peoples, dreams carry warnings (*DBNP* 66, *SRC* 249), furnish answers to personal questions (*WIB* 95), help to formulate one's personal identity (*WIB* 95), are the source of new names (*TPY* 54), provide guidance as to whom one should trust (*TPY* 44), convey information about hunting (*TPY* 181), and help to locate missing loved ones (*GOS* 211).

In *GOS*, the highly respected leader Red Thunder, a member of the party whose rescue was made possible by Omakayas's dream, acknowledges the high value placed on dreams and dreamers among Ojibwe people when he tells Omakayas that the ability to dream is a very great gift bestowed on her by the Great Spirit Gizhe Manidoo (221).

Valuing Sharing and Peaceful Relations With Neighboring Nations

A prominent individual in three novels identifies the value of sharing or peaceful relations with neighboring people for Inuit, Lakota, or Mohawk people. In *COTS*, The-man-with-no-eyebrows acknowledges the importance for Inuit people of sharing their personal possessions with each other, food and other necessities (35, 50). In *LLM*, while teaching a traditional Lakota dance to students at Lori's school, a local hoop dancer named High Eagle stresses the importance for Lakota people of sharing dance hoops with each other (37).

In *COTL*, Ohkwa'ri overhears some local boys planning an unauthorized raid on a neighboring Abenaki village during the Mohawk strawberry harvest and reflects on the high value placed on peaceful relations with these neighbors by his village leaders (7).

Acting Calmly, Humbly, and Honorably

A prominent individual in three novels identifies the cultural value of calmness, humility, or honor for Narraganset, Ojibwe, or Mohawk peoples. In *WITD*, Maddy recalls an important lesson about calmness conveyed by traditional Narraganset stories (112–14). As she rushes into the local library with her friend Roger to check on her aunt, who works at the library and may be missing, she recalls the Narraganset value of keeping calm in the face of danger. In chapters 17 and 21, she first reminds herself that you can only think clearly when you are calm (114), then tells herself to be calm (138).

In *TPY* chapter 14, Omakayas's grandmother Nokomis speaks sharply to her daughter Muskrat with other family members present about the importance of humility—the quality of being humble (152). The online *American Heritage Dictionary* defines humble as marked by meekness or modesty in behavior, attitude, or spirit; not arrogant or prideful.[2] Nokomis contrasts Old Tallow's humble action (sacrificing herself for the family) with her granddaughter Two Strike's arrogant action (knocking a cup of hot tea from her aunt Yellow Kettle's hand).

In *COTL* chapter 1, Ohkwa'ri reflects twice on the importance of honor for Mohawk people. First he reflects on important positions of honor in his village, collectively called the *Roia:ne* in Mohawk. The online *Oxford English Dictionary* defines honor as great respect or esteem gained or enjoyed by a person.[3] Ohkwa'ri identifies three positions of honor in his village: the Faith

Keeper, Pine Tree Chief, and leaders of men. These individuals, described by Ohkwa'ri as wise and careful, never went to war, killed people, nor stole from people (9). Ohkwa'ri also reflects on the honor gained by Mohawk warriors in battle (14–15).

Respecting Others

Respecting others is an important value for Mohawk people. According to the online *American Heritage Dictionary,* to show respect means to feel or show deferential regard for.[4] In *COTL* members of the Mohawk Flint Nation are respected by members of the Abenaki Nation (7) and rise to leadership positions by securing the respect of members of their community (8).

Respecting animals is an important value for Ojibwe, Abenaki-Mohican, and Shawnee peoples. Prominent individuals in three novels behave respectfully towards animals encountered in their homeland and elsewhere. Omakayas, Sonny, and Armie have respectful encounters with black bears (*TPY* 35), deer (*HR* 36), a cross fox (*DP* 20–24), and birds—a robin and chickadees (*DP* 13–15).

6. CULTURAL EVENTS

The identification of traditional Indigenous events focusing on a game, dance, song, dancing or singing, a feast, festival, or ceremony is a distinguishing feature of indigenized fictional worlds. Prominent individuals in 12 novels identify and describe in varying detail one or more of these cultural events.

SET 6.1 TRADITIONAL GAMES, DANCING, AND SONGS

A prominent individual in 11 novels identifies a traditional game, dance, category of dancer, song, or singing event that is important for Mohawk, Ojibwe, Inuit, Sto: loh, Shawnee, Choctaw, Lakota, or Abenaki people.

Traditional Games

Traditional games are identified in seven novels. Half or more of these games are played with objects (e.g., sticks, balls, carved pieces of wood, bones). Game participants may be largely stationary, as in the game of snow snakes, or may spend a considerable amount of time running within a marked area.

Stationary games include the spear and hoop, deer knuckle, arm twisting, and Lahal games identified in *COTL* (50), *GOS* (17), *COTS* (152), and *WG* (35); the snow snake game described in *COTL* (114–15) and *GOS* (165); and the game of silence described in *GOS* (12–15).

Running games include toss and catch described in *COTS* (41), tag and soccer identified in *COTS* (41, 153), and various stick and ball games identified or described in *DP* (117), *SRC* (256), and *COTL* (4, 90–95). Wrestling, a game that engages two individuals in continuous physical contact, is identified in *COTL* (98) and *COTS* (152), and rope gymnastics is described briefly in *COTS* (152).

Toss and Catch

The traditional Inuit game of toss and catch is described in *COTS* (41). The game is played with two teams of players and a small sack of sand. Players on each team aim not to be caught with the sack by players on the opposite team, so players move quickly around the playing field, tossing the sack back and forth among themselves.

Stick and Ball Games

A prominent individual in two novels identifies traditional stick and ball games played by Choctaw or Shawnee people. In *SCR*, after an exhausting two-hour game of stick-ball, Koi Losa collapses in the grass and recounts his recent experience disposing of a witch owl, an evil Choctaw spirit (256). In *DP*, Armie recalls the traditional stick and ball games played by his Shawnee ancestors, a game similar to present-day lacrosse (117).

Various historical accounts of a popular Choctaw stick and ball game known as the two-stick (racket) game are assembled by Swanton (1931). According to these accounts, the Choctaw two-stick game was a match between two village teams that concluded when one team reached the end score of 100 points. Playing sticks made of walnut or chestnut wood were held in each player's hands. These sticks, whose ends were bent into oblong shapes and meshed to trap the game ball, measured two and a half feet in length. Fairly large goals were erected at each end of the playing field.

A game got underway when an old man threw up the game ball, and players from each village team vigorously sought to catch the ball with the meshed ends of their sticks, toss the ball to a teammate, move the ball downfield, and score a goal. Bossu (1768) and Romans (1775) report that teams of women played the two-stick game as well. A male game uniform consisted of a breach-cloth, beaded belt, neck ornamentation, and a tail made of white horsehair or quills (see Swanton plate 4).

The Mohawk game stick used in the popular stick and ball game *Tekwaarathon* is shown on the front cover of *COTL*. Brief and detailed information about this traditional Mohawk game is provided by Ohkwa'ri and Otsi:stia in the first and second parts of the novel. Brief information about the game is provided by Ohkwa'ri in chapter 1 and Otsi:stia in chapter 7. Details about the game's origins, players, game sticks, and game preparations are provided in chapters 8–11. Details from an actual game and the outcome of that game are provided in chapters 11–13 and the epilogue.

Snow Snakes

A prominent individual in two novels identifies and describes the traditional game of snow snakes played in the wintertime by Ojibwe and Mohawk peoples. In *GOS*, Omakayas identifies the Ojibwe snow snake game sticks as snakes, the ornamentation of these snakes, Ojibwe children like herself as typical players, and the playing field as long stretches of lake ice (165). In *COTL*, Otsi:stia describes Mohawk snow snake sticks as long spear-like poles with painted eyes and the playing field as troughs of snow (114–15).

Game of Silence

In *GOS* chapter 2, confined to their small birchbark house for a fourth rainy day, Omakayas and her little brother Pinch each endeavors to beat the other in a traditional game of silence (12–15). As Omakayas notes, the first player to break the silence loses. Although repeatedly tempted to laugh at or scold her brother for his various antics (making faces at her, stealing her doll, poking the fire), Omakayas imagines herself to be a stone, silent and immovable, and maintains her composure and silence. Their game ends in a draw when some visitors drop by unexpectedly.

Traditional Dances and Dancers

Traditional dances are identified in five novels. These dances include the hoop dance (*LLM* 35–37), the round dance (*LLM* 70, *MT* 36), the grass dance (*LLM* 92, *WG* 23), the fancy dance (*WG* 23), the thunder dance (*COTL* 26), the moon dance (*COTL* 26–27), the harvest dance (*COTL* 27), and the winter gathering dance (*BH* 129, 140–42). Jingle dancers are identified by Lori during her fall visit to Custer State Park in *LLM* (94), and prominent individuals in three novels participate in a round dance, a winter gathering dance, or a hoop dance.

Jingle (Dress) Dancers

Jingle (dress) dancers are popular performers at powwows across the United States and Canada. A powwow is a special event, hosted by North American Indigenous peoples, that celebrates their distinctive identities and cultures, past and present. Indigenous peoples from many parts of both countries, the United States and Canada, gather to dance, sing, and pray in traditional ways. During a traditional jingle dance, a jingle dancer's dress, lined with rows of metal cones, produces a soothing sound that mimics rain.

In *LLM*, Lori and her sister Lana watch the jingle dancers perform at a powwow held at Custer State Park in October. During the first part of dance, the announcer talks about the origins of the dance and its birthplace on an Ojibwe reservation (94–95).

Harvest, Thunder, and Moon Dances

Members of the Mohawk Nation in *COTL* hold harvest, thunder, and moon dances to "mark the end of the summer," "herald the return of those loud-voiced sky beings who are the friends of the people and bring the rain to nurture and cleans the earth," and "giv[e] thanks to our grandmother who watches over the night skies" (26–27).

Hoop Dance

In *LLM*, the Lakota hoop dancer High Eagle shares his hoops with students at Lori's school, and both Lori and her sister Lana try their hand at traditional hoop dancing for the first time. Before Lori, Lana, and the other students are invited to dance, High Eagle explains the meaning of each hoop, then puts the hoops to use in the context of dancing. Lori observes him carefully and notes the way he flips the hoops upward with his feet, spins the hoops on his arms and legs, assembles them in one united intricate form, and returns them to the floor (35–36).

Hoop dancing takes considerable skill to perform, as Lori soon learns. She easily spins one hoop around her waist, but struggles to spin even one hoop on her arm. Lana is more successful than her sister at first, managing to twirl several hoops on her arms and to flip one onto her leg, but she quickly loses control of the hoops (37).

The Grass Dance

The defining feature of the modern North American Indigenous grass dance is not the dancer's movements but rather the fringed elements in the dancer's costume. Both upper and lower parts of the grass dancer's costume contain brightly colored fringes made from yarn, fabric, or ribbon. According to Howard (1951), the grass dance originated among the warrior societies of the northern Great Plains region.

Grass dance costumes are simply identified or described by prominent individuals in two novels. In *WG*, Will simply identifies his own grass dance outfit (23). In *LLM*, Lori describes the memorable fringed costumes worn by the grass dancers at the Custer State Park powwow whose colorful fringes swayed like grass in the wind (92).

Fancy Dance

According to Ellis (2003), the fancy dance was created and popularized in the early 20th century by members of the Ponca Nation, an Indigenous Nation from the Midwest region of the United States now situated in Nebraska and Oklahoma. Then and now, the fancy dance is a highly spirited dance performed by young men and boys whose costumes are distinguished by twin feather bustles and bells worn just below the knees.

The fancy shawl dance, performed by female dancers, evolved from the original fancy dance performed by male dancers. This recently conceived version of the fancy dance enacts the emergence of a butterfly from a cocoon. Female fancy dance costumes are distinguished by a colorful fringed shawl decorated with embroidery or ribbon. Female fancy dancers commonly wear beaded hairpieces, chokers, earrings, bracelets, and eagle plumes.

In *WG*, Will identifies both male and female fancy dance costumes, one belonging to him and one belonging to his aunt Sarah (23).

Winter Gathering Dance

In *BH*, a winter gathering dance is held at the great dance lodge in LaPointe on the Island of the Golden-Breasted Woodpecker (140–42). As always, the dance lodge is crowded with people, old people and young people. Angeline arrives at the dance lodge early wearing her new shawl decorated with thimbles and ribbons (129–31), and is among the first young women to begin dancing, bouncing gracefully to the drum beat, holding her new dance fan.

Traditional Songs and Singing

Traditional songs are heard, sung, or recited by prominent individuals in six novels. In *TPY* and *GOS*, Omakayas sings various traditional songs while traveling by canoe. In *TPY*, as she travels across the lake by canoe, she and her family members sing traveling songs, surprise songs, nonsense songs, and love songs (60).

In *GOS*, as Omakayas and her family members travel northward by canoe to their new home many miles away, everyone sings the traditional traveling songs that help to keep them hopeful and their paddling coordinated (247); and when their route gets dangerous while traveling downriver, Omakayas hears her grandmother in the next canoe singing the song that introduces the game of silence (247).

In *WP*, Saxso sings traditional songs twice while traveling by canoe. While fleeing from his attackers at night with a kinsman, he sings a traditional paddling song jointly addressed to himself and the underwater people (46). Then traveling alone en route to rescue his mother and sisters, he sings an old Abenaki song, taught to him by his father, as he paddles along the river that loves old Abenaki songs.

Also in *WP*, Saxso hears members of his village singing shortly before a nighttime attack by British forces that devastates the village. One kinsman sings the greeting song, and a young girl sings a traditional lament (33, 41–42).

Traditional berry picking songs and traditional songs performed at a special event are heard by Will while dreaming in *WG*. In one dream Will hears his ancestors singing traditional songs in the mountains while picking blueberries, and in another he hears his kinsmen performing various traditional songs at a national exhibition in Vancouver, British Columbia (5, 35).

A traditional childhood song focusing alternately on a child's life in future and present time is recited twice in *COTS*, once in a shorter form in chapter 9 and once in a longer form in chapter 22. In chapter 9, Wolverine sings the song himself, first singing about his life in future time—being big and traveling about with his father—then singing about his life in present time—being small and staying home with his mother (37). In chapter 22, now a young man recently returned from his captivity on Marble Island, Wolverine hears his mother singing the full version of this childhood song (142).

Moreover, in the last chapter of *COTS*, a traditional song is chanted by the people who are gathered in the party igloo at the Spring Festival. This traditional song speaks of happy and wondrous times for Inuit people, a shining moon in the nighttime sky, a dog team and sled traveling on the snow, a beautiful inlet in the distance, and special animals that inhabit the frozen landscape—"*Aijaa . . . jijja quvianaqquuq*" (151–52).

In *COTL*, Otsi:stia sings a traditional lullaby while holding a cradleboard flower: "'Little One in your cradleboard,'" she sings, "'. . . your mother has hung you here from a tree limb. Now as the wind comes, your cradleboard sways. Sleep, little one, sleep'" (54).

SET 6.2 FAMILY-BASED FEASTS

The same prominent individual in two novels, Omakayas, identifies family-based feasts that have traditional importance for Ojibwe people.

Special Celebratory Event Feasts

Special celebratory event feasts, described by Omakayas, are held in two *Birchbark House* series novels. A homecoming feast especially for her father Deydey is held in *BH* chapter 4, and another homecoming feast, celebrating the safe return of her father and Father Baraga, is held in *GOS* chapter 14. At this latter feast in *GOS*, Omakayas's newfound ability as a dreamer is also celebrated (60).

In *BH*, in preparation for the special homecoming feast for Deydey later that day, Omakayas and her sister Angeline use their grandmother's fishing net to capture and kill some tasty red-winged blackbirds for their meal (56–58). The two sisters cleverly trap the birds with the net, and Omakayas looks away from her sister when she catches hold of each bird in the net and breaks its neck with a quick snapping motion. Their mother covers the birds with mud and cooks them under burning coals with wild onions.

The special homecoming feast for Deydey in *BH* includes a meal, storytelling, and gift-giving. The homecoming meal consists of roasted blackbirds, roasted ears of corn, sweet blueberries, and a strong tea made from wintergreen leaves (60). After the meal, Deydey and Omakayas's grandmother both smoke pipes, and Deydey shares an exhilarating story about a personal encounter with cannibal ghosts (61–67). To end the feast, Deydey gives each member of the family a special gift (68).

Naming Feasts

In *TPY* chapter 5, a traditional Ojibwe naming feast is held for Omakayas after she demonstrates extraordinary courage one morning, wrestling an eagle (51–57). She waits for the eagle under the drying rack, lures the eagle with deer meat, grabs the eagle by the tail, wrestles with it fiercely—is observed by her father Deydey, emerging from the woods—and is rewarded with two magnificent tail feathers and a naming feast.

Omakayas's naming feast is held the next day and begins with a purifying sweat. Everyone pitches in to construct a sweat lodge. The women and girls purify themselves first, then the men and boys. Deydey, still in the sweat lodge, summons his daughter to the doorway, shares his recent dream with her, and gives her the new name of Ogimabineskiwe (Leading Thunderbird

Woman in Ojibwe), his grandmother's name. Today's special feast consists of venison stew and softened roots fried in beavertail grease.

SET 6.3 FESTIVALS AND SPECIAL COMMUNITY EVENTS

A traditional Inuit, Mohawk, or Abenaki festival, game, or dance is identified in four novels. The Great Mohawk Ball Game (*Tekwaarathon*, see "Traditional Games") and important Mohawk festivals including the Strawberry and Maple Festivals are described in detail or simply identified in *COTL*. The novel *COTS* closes with a detailed account of an Inuit Spring Festival, and the novel *WP* opens with a description provided by Saxso of an Abenaki celebratory dance held at the Council Hall in his village.

Strawberry Festival, Maple Festival, and Corn Harvest

In *COTL* chapter 2, Otsi:stia notes key details about the traditional Strawberry Festival held in her village and celebrated by all Mohawk people (23–28). The festival gets underway in early morning with a special Thanksgiving Address delivered by her uncle Big Tree (see chapter 4, "Addressing Skonkwaiatison").

Following the address, a group of singers settles on fireside seats and sings traditional Mohawk songs accompanied by drums and rattles. Soon Otsi:stia finds herself on the dance floor, dancing rhythmically to a unified drum beat with her mother, grandmother, and other members of the ancient women's circle of blessing and thanks, all celebrating the new strawberry harvest.

The Mohawk Maple Festival is simply identified by Otsi:stia in *COTL* chapter 2 (26). According to the *Haudenosaunee Guide For Educators* (National Museum of the American Indian 2009), in the Haudenosaunee calendar, the Maple Festival honors the sap that flows from maple trees each spring.

Spring Festival

An important Inuit spring festival, attended by The-man-with-no-eyebrows, Paaliaq, their wives and children, and other Inuit families, is held at Bit-of-Sand in *COTS* chapter 23 (146–54). Paaliaq announces the special springtime event and oversees the building of a large festival igloo. The festival lasts for many days and nights and gives people many opportunities to play traditional Inuit games, share stories about their recent wintertime experiences, sing, dance, make special announcements, and give special gifts.

Celebratory Dance

In *WP* chapters 1–4, a traditional Abenaki dance celebrating the first frost, a bountiful harvest, an abundant supply of deer meat, and a recent wedding is held at the big Council Hall in Saxso's home village of St. Francis (6–7, 18–34). Tonight's traditional celebratory dance begins unremarkably. People drink cider freely, join hands, stomp along the dance floor to the rhythmic beat of drums, and sing traditional songs of celebration and friendship. But tonight's dance ends remarkably early for a troubling reason.

SET 6.4 CEREMONIES

A ceremony is defined by the online *American Heritage Dictionary* as a formal act or set of acts performed as prescribed by ritual or custom.[5] Community, family-based, and individual events are specifically identified as traditional ceremonies in seven novels.

Three annual Mohawk ceremonies held by members of Otsi:stia's community are identified in *COTL*: the midwinter ceremony, which follows the strawberry festival; the planting ceremony; and the seasons ceremony that marks the endpoint of another cycle of seasons (26–27). Traditional coming-of-age ceremonies for young Ojibwe women and young Sto: loh men are identified in *TPY* (107) and *WG* (12); a Choctaw naming ceremony is identified in *NMNN* (24); and detailed accounts of a Lakota naming ceremony, a Sto: loh Becoming Man Ceremony, and traditional wedding ceremonies held for Choctaw and Inuit couples appear in *LLM*, *WG*, *COTS*, and *SRC*.

Lakota Naming Ceremony

In *LLM*, Lori and Lana learn about a traditional naming ceremony held in the past for all Lakota children when they reached puberty (26–27, 30). The two cousins also learn about traditional Lakota names like All-Around Medicine Woman and Moving Woman—names used by their maternal and paternal grandmothers (Pejuta Okawin and Skanskanwin in Lakota). According to their grandmother and her friend, the circumstances of one's birth often determined the first name a child received (e.g., Red Leaf, born in autumn); and for the past 100 years or so, recipients of new names were given quilts that celebrated special events in their lives.

Choctaw Wedding Ceremony

In *SRC* chapter 48, an older Choctaw couple, Funi Man and Shonti, are married in a traditional Choctaw wedding ceremony. Seven elements in this traditional Choctaw ceremony are described in chapter 48. These elements include the chase, attire, circling, singing, dancing, a blessing, and feasting.

The marriage in chapter 48 is endorsed by the Choctaw Council and residents of Choctaw town [*sic*] and permitted to proceed when the traditional wedding chase ends with the bride-to-be being caught by the groom-to-be in a spirited race towards the wedding pole (see *SRC* chapter 4, pp. 18–20). People turn out in great numbers to witness the chase. Local people and visitors attend the event in colorful shirts and skirts (288–96).

The ceremony continues with the couple joining hands and forming a circle around the wedding pole. On this particular occasion, as described in chapter 48, another couple, Martha Tom and Lil Mo, joins hands with the bride and groom and forms a circle of four around the wedding pole. To this stationary inner circle is added a moving outer circle of dancers, all holding hands and moving silently like ducks and deer. All sing the Choctaw wedding chant to celebrate the marriage of Funi Man and Shonti and the betrothal of Martha Tom and Lil Mo, then the wedding couple is blessed by the tribal pastor.

The wedding ceremony concludes with a feast that lasts until morning. All in attendance help themselves to generous portions of soup, meat, and pudding.

Inuit Wedding Ceremony

In the closing chapter of the novel *COTS*, a traditional Inuit wedding ceremony is held for Wolverine and Breath at Bit-of-sand, the location of the Spring Festival (149–51). Breath's father Paaliaq announces the wedding in the large festival igloo and wishes his daughter and new son-in-law much happiness and many children. The couple receives gifts of a sled and dogs from their parents, holds hands, and calls each other wife and husband before retiring to a small connecting igloo to spend time with each other alone.

A wedding feast, singing, and dancing follows. Everyone contributes food for the feast. Plates of meat and steaming pots of soup are passed from person to person in the festival igloo. A drum is restrung, tuned, and played, which prompts the song described above in the section "Traditional Songs and Singing."

Sto: loh Becoming Man Ceremony

In *WG* chapter 12, Will gives a detailed account of his Becoming Man Ceremony, an event that occupies his thoughts off and on from the opening chapter of the novel. As described by Will in chapter 12, this traditional Sto: loh event helps young Sto: loh men like Will to transition from childhood to adulthood through prayer, purification, personal mementos, sacred objects, meaningful reflection, public acknowledgments, promises, gift-giving, music, singing, and feasting. Will's ceremony begins at sunrise, spans roughly half the day, and requires Will to spend time at three key locations in his community (119–28).

Will's Becoming Man Ceremony begins at home. He rises with the sun and joins his parents and siblings in the yard for a family prayer that focuses partly on Will and partly on his parents and siblings. His father delivers the prayer for the family, speaks to the sun about the importance of his family and the forthcoming changes in their lives, and offers to the world his last son Will with an offering of tobacco. Everyone joins Will's father singing, then Will heads to the river for a purifying sweat with his father, grandfather, brother-in-law, and other male members of his family.

Later that morning, Will heads to the community longhouse for the last part of his Becoming Man Ceremony. He arrives at this last ceremonial location with several childhood photographs and four ceremonial objects. The photographs show him with different family members, all noteworthy people in his life. His ceremonial objects include a stone, a crow feather, an eagle claw, and a sprig of cedar. Will looks around the longhouse. Many people have turned out for this special event.

Will's relatives and friends are seated on benches by the fire. Will stands next to them, plants his feet firmly on the ground, arranges his photographs in front of him, and between drumrolls publicly acknowledges each person that appears with him in a photograph—his mother, sister, aunt, and grandmother. He acknowledges his sister's son, who bears his name; thanks the men in his family for lightening his load; acknowledges his responsibility to the community and role as a caretaker of the land; and states his career goal. Will's Becoming Man Ceremony ends with a midday feast.

NOTES

1. American Heritage Dictionary, s.v. "dream (n.)," accessed February 4, 2023, https://www.ahdictionary.com/dream.

2. American Heritage Dictionary, s.v. "humble (n.)," accessed February 4, 2023, https://www.ahdictionary.com/humble.

3. Oxford English Dictionary, s.v. "honor (n.)," accessed February 4, 2023, https://www.oed.com /honour.

4. American Heritage Dictionary, s.v. "respect (n.)," accessed February 4, 2023, https://www.ahdictionary.com/respect.

5. American Heritage Dictionary, s.v. "ceremony (n.)," accessed February 4, 2023, https://www.ahdictionary.com/ceremony.

REFERENCES

Bossu, M. *Nouveaux Voyages aux Index Occidentales.* Vols. I–II. Paris, 1768.

Ellis, Clyde. *A Dancing People: Powwow Culture on the Southern Plains.* Lawrence: University of Kansas Press, 2003.

Howard, James. "Notes on the Dakota Grass Dance." *Southwestern Journal of Anthropology* 7 no. 1 (1951): 82–85.

National Museum of the American Indian (NMAI). *Haudenosaunee Guide For Educators.* Washington, DC: Smithsonian, 2009.

Romans, B. *A Concise Natural History of East and West Florida.* Vol. 1. New York, 1775.

Swanton, John R. *Source Material for the Social and Ceremonial Life of the Choctaw Indians.* Washington, DC: United States Government Printing Office, 1931.

Chapter 6

Group B

Cultural Traditions

CHAPTER OVERVIEW

Indigenizing fictional world features in Group B and the Category of Cultural Traditions are examined in this chapter. Seven sets of Category 7 features are examined. In all, 40 indigenizing features are identified, described, and illustrated in this chapter.

7. Cultural Traditions
   7.1 Traditional knowledge, skills, and roles: traditional knowledge about local wildlife, traditional skills (outdoor fire-making), traditional roles
   7.2 Subsistence strategies: large game hunting, rabbit hunting, bird hunting, sharing, trapping, fishing, clamming, whaling, herding, tracking, plant and wild rice harvesting
   7.3 Traditional modes of travel and conveyance: water travel, snow travel, infant travel, stealth
   7.4 Traditional houses and shelters: traditional houses, traditional shelters
   7.5 Traditional craftsmanship and repairs: house and shelter building, boat building and repair, net making, tanning, traditional clothes and clothing accessories, blankets and blanket making, mats and baskets, wood carving, ornamentation, toy making
   7.6 Traditional implements and materials: traditional implements, traditional weapons, traditional materials
   7.7 Traditional foods, drinks, and medicines: traditional foods, traditional drinks, traditional medicines, food preparation, food storage

7. CULTURAL TRADITIONS

Cultural traditions focusing on traditional Indigenous knowledge or roles, subsistence strategies, modes of transportation, housing, craftsmanship, implements, medicines, food preparation, and more are identified and described in varying detail by prominent individuals in 23 novels. Cultural traditions are distinguishing features of indigenized fictional worlds.

SET 7.1 TRADITIONAL KNOWLEDGE, SKILLS, AND ROLES

Traditional Knowledge About Local Wildlife

In *COTS*, Breath learns about the seasonal movements of caribou from her mother, as thousands of caribou pass by their encampment in the spring, heading north. Breath learns from her mother that the caribou are traveling inland to calve. Her mother tells her that caribou are similar to humans by wanting to give birth to their babies in a safe place: "They go back to that same place every year where they can keep an eye on the wolves that are always after their babies," says her mother (105).

In *TPY*, Omakayas uses her traditional knowledge about bears to protect her brother Bizheens from two scruffy bears while picking strawberries in the woods one day with her mother and grandmother (31–36). Omakayas has knowledge about bears. She learned at a very young age that bears were unpredictable and dangerous, fearing people at times and killing them at times (typically children) for food. She is well aware that bears were especially dangerous in early summer when their stores of winter fat were depleted and berries were just beginning to ripen.

The two bears stare hungrily at Bizheens from the leafy edge of the woods, sizing him up as a meal. Omakayas springs into action. She intercepts the bears, jumps in front of Bizheens, stops him from advancing with her leg, and waves her arms wildly in the air to make herself look large and threatening. She orders the bears to go, telling them that Bizheens is her little brother, and they should be ashamed to regard him as food.

Traditional Skills: Outdoor Fire-Making

Prominent individuals in two novels use their fire-making skills in the woods. In *HR*, Sonny uses his traditional fire-making skills while on a spiritual wilderness outing with his uncle (62). In *DP*, Armie makes a fire in the old

Shawnee way while waiting for something to reveal itself by the dark pond in the forest (54–55).

Traditional Roles

Traditional roles identified in nine novels include the hunter (*TPY* 63, *LLM* 15), trapper (*MT* 21), holy man (*LLM*), healer (*TPY* 104), medicine man (*HTS* 95, *BH* 75), medicine woman (*LV* 245), shaman (*DP* 104, *COTS* 10), warrior (*NN* 65, *TPY* 17, 20, 53, 152), war captain (*COTL* 14), scout (*NN* 62), orator (*COTL* 52), and storyteller (*COTS* 11). Specific leadership roles (e.g., chief, clan mother) are discussed in chapter 9.

SET 7.2 SUBSISTENCE STRATEGIES

Large Game Hunting

Prominent living and deceased individuals in eight novels routinely hunt or hunted large game near their homes for food. Large game animals include moose (*TPY* 132, *LV* 67, *HTS* 189, *MT* 48, *GOS* 79), deer (*LLM* 15, *MT* 45), caribou (*COTS* 46, *TPY* 132), bison (i.e., buffalo, *LLM* 79), black bears (*BH* 35), polar bears (*COTS* 12), seals (*COTS* 12), and walruses (*COTS* 93).

Rabbit Hunting

Prominent individuals in *TPY* and *COTS* hunt rabbits for food. In *TPY* Animikiins and his father return from hunting with a couple of fat rabbits (likely snowshoe hares, 40), and in *COTS* The-man-with-no-eyebrows and other members of his group travel inland in early winter to hunt arctic hares (*COTS* 46).

Bird Hunting

Prominent individuals in three novels hunt geese (*TPY* 164), ptarmigan (*COTS* 46), and partridges (*HTS* 53, 143). The geese identified in *TPY* may be Canada Geese, Cackling Geese, or Greater White-fronted Geese. Residents of northern Ontario commonly call the Ruffed Grouse a partridge.

Snaring

Prominent individuals in five novels snare a small game animal or game birds for food. Snared rabbits and partridges are important sources of food during the winter months for individuals or groups of people in *TPY* (12), *LV* (39, 211), *HTS* (124, 144), *SW* (135), and *BH* (145). As previously noted, the partridges identified in *LV* (211) and *HTS* (144) are likely Ruffed Grouse.

Trapping

Prominent individuals in four novels spend time, have spent time, or have family friends that spend time on a trapline. A trapline or trapline cabin is identified in *MT* (20), *BH* (74), *HTS* (11), and *LV* (42). Beavers and marten are trapped in *TPY* (151) and *SW* (235). In *SW*, Ol' Jim hangs stretched animal skins from the rafters of his trapline cabin (206), and in *LV* an old Ojibwe man speaks to Ray and her classmates about beaver traps, other types of traps, and trapping activities in the summer, spring, winter, and fall (67–68).

Fishing

Prominent individuals in seven novels catch a variety of fish species including pickerel (*HTS* 20, *SW* 115), whitefish (*BH* 190), suckers (*HTS* 20, *SW* 115), trout (*TPY* 76, *BH* 190), sturgeon (*SW* 159), and pike (commonly called jackfish, *HTS* 20, *SW* 125, *LV* 237, *GOS* 189). Prominent individuals in *COTS* are specifically identified as fisherpersons and fishers (87–88).

Various fishing techniques, fishing activities, and fishing gear are identified in six novels. Identified fishing techniques include spearfishing (*COTS* 87–88, *GOS* 189), netting (*LV* 51, *HTS* 19, *GOS* 110, *WG* 32), angling with rods (*SW* 75), angling with a hook and line (*HTS* 25, *SW* 125), and weir trapping (*COTS* 87). Identified fishing activities include checking a net (*SW* 110–11), spearing a fish (*COTS* 87–88), and the generic activity of fishing (*WG* 17). Winter fishing is identified in *BH* (132) and *GOS* (189), and in *COTS* identified fishing gear includes decoys and spears (87–88).

Clamming

In *WG*, Will recalls a childhood memory about clamming in a dream (35).

Whaling

In *COTS*, various Inuit hunters including The-man-with-no-eyebrows and his only son Wolverine engage in whaling. These Inuit hunters pursue beluga whales (86) and bowhead whales (106, 110).

Herding

In two novels in the *Danny Blackgoat* series, Danny Blackgoat herds sheep before his capture (*DBNP* 1–4) and later in captivity recalls his activities as a sheep herder back in his homeland (*DBDP* 5). In the opening pages of the first novel *DBNP*, Danny awakens before sunrise, leads his family's flock of 24 sheep from the corral to the end of the canyon, climbs a steep path to a higher elevation, gazes down at his house, and recites a prayer taught to him by his grandfather.

Tracking

Prominent individuals in five novels encounter and identify local wildlife tracks close to home or while traveling by foot in dry, wet, or snowy wilderness locations. Tracked animals include deer (*LLM* 10, *MT* 45, *DP* 25), rabbits (*LLM* 10, *GOS* 171, *DP* 25), wolf (*WP* 118), grouse (*DP* 25), mice (*DP* 25), and voles (*DP* 25).

Prominent individuals in two novels seek to locate adversaries and recover loved ones by tracking human or animal footprints. In *WP* and *DBRRTF*, Saxso and Danny Blackgoat seek to recover their mother, sisters, or fiance by tracking their loved ones' captors on foot or horseback. Saxso's mother and sisters are captured by Bostonian Rangers (118, 123) and Danny Blackgoat's fiance by slave traders (124–25).

Plant and Wild Rice Harvesting

Prominent individuals in four novels engage in plant cultivation or wild rice harvesting. Cultivated plants include strawberries (*COTL* 9), the Indigenous North American three sister crops of corn, bean, and squash (*COTL* 22), corn/squash (*BH* 226, *TPY* 127), and pumpkin (*BH* 226). In *BH* and *GOS*, Omakayas and her family members harvest wild rice in their seasonal wild rice harvesting location (9, 74).

SET 7.3 TRADITIONAL MODES OF
TRAVEL AND CONVEYANCE

Water Travel

Prominent individuals in 11 novels travel to and from various locations by kayak or canoe when local water routes are not obstructed by ice. In *COTS*, Wolverine and his father travel by kayak to a famous island to hunt whales

(110), and when the sea is clear of ice Wolverine attempts to travel home alone by kayak (114, 133).

Prominent individuals in seven novels hunt by canoe (*TPY* 1–8), catch fish by canoe using nets or rods (*LV* 182, 229, *HTS* 19–20, 57, *SW* 75, 110–11, 115, 125), harvest wild rice by canoe (*BH* 95–96, *GOS* 74, 82), travel by canoe to visit relatives or family friends (*SW* 93–178, *LV* 164–66), travel by canoe to buy groceries or other necessities at a distant store (*LV* 231), observe men paddling a canoe (*LV* 50–51), or spot canoes traveling along a river (*COTL* 46–47).

In *LV*, *WITD*, and *MTTT* respectively, Ray, Maddy, and Louis travel by canoe for the first time (*LV* 43–46), imagine crossing paths with an ancestor traveling by canoe (*WITD* 97–98), and dream about approaching rapids by canoe (*MTTT* 26). At the start and end of *GOS*, Omakayas and her family welcome a ragged group of Ojibwe travelers, traveling southward by canoe (prologue), then leave their cherished island by canoe, searching for a new life northward (246–48).

In *LV* and *WP*, Ray and Saxso have no means of traveling home or crossing rivers safely other than by canoe (*WP* 46–47, 51, *LV* 184). In *WP*, Saxso travels eastward by canoe in pursuit of his captured mother and sisters (96–109, 152–55).

Canoeing destinations in five novels include seasonal campsites (*LV* 36–39), short-term campsites (*BH* 94, *GOS* 75), notable islands (*LV* 234), locations where wild blueberries grow abundantly (*LV* 150–54, 182), and trading posts (*BH* 2, 9). In *LV* various portages are required when traveling by canoe.

Snow Travel

Prominent individuals in seven novels routinely use dog teams and sleds, toboggans, sleighs, snowshoes, snowmobiles, and traditional eye gear for seasonal travel when local land and water routes are frozen and covered with snow. These individuals travel to and from winter cabins or hunt using a dog team and sled (*LV* 221, *COTS* 12), move camp using a dog team and sled or toboggan (*COTS* 15, 47–50, *BH* 108), and transport people, firewood, groceries, or camp gear using a dog team, dogsled, toboggan, snowmobile, or sleigh (*GOS* 176, *LV* 221, *HTS* 174, *SW* 217).

Prominent individuals in five novels travel by snowshoe (*LV* 217, *BH* 194, *TPY* 136, *GOS* 165, *SW* 235), and in *COTS* The-man-with-no-eyebrows wears traditional wooden goggles with tiny slits to prevent snow blindness (38).

Infant Travel

Traditional Ojibwe cradleboards, constructed and decorated by family members, are used to transport infants by land in *BH* (43, 92) and *GOS* (9).

Stealth

In *HR* and *WP*, Sonny and Saxso both move stealthily to avoid detection. Sonny copies his uncle and moves through the woods stealthily with a "careful, slow stride that hardly rustled the leaves" so as not to startle wildlife (19). Saxso crawls stealthily through the woods, inching closer to his adversaries' campsite, where his mother and sister are being held as captives (123).

SET 7.4 TRADITIONAL HOUSES AND SHELTERS

Traditional Houses

Prominent individuals in 10 novels live in traditional houses seasonally or permanently. Traditional houses identified in these novels include igloos (*COTS* 2), longhouses (*SM* 3, *COTL* 19–20, *WP* 25), birchbark wigwams or lodges (*WP* 20, *BH* 6, 91, *MT* 22, *GOS* 16), hogans (*DBDP* 5), log cabins (*LV* 65, *WP* 26), square timber houses (*WP* 26), one-room cabins (*HTS* 11), cedar cabins (*BH* 6), and winter cabins (*BH* 100, *GOS* 97).

Traditional Shelters

Omakayas, Saxso, Ohkwa'ri, Ray, and Lori spend time in one or more traditional shelters including a sugar house (*BH* 212), small hunting wigwam (*WP* 26), one-person lodge (*COTL* 43–52), canvas tent (*LV* 154), sweat lodge (*GOS* 117, *TPY* 54), or lean-to (*GOS* 75). A hunting tipi is identified in *LLM* (70).

SET 7.5 TRADITIONAL CRAFTSMANSHIP AND REPAIRS

House and Shelter Building

Prominent individuals in five novels work together or alone to build a traditional Inuit, Ojibwe, or Mohawk house or shelter. In *COTS*, Wolverine's father and future father-in-law work together to build a new igloo for Wolverine's family (32–35). In all three *Birchbark House* series novels,

Omakayas, her family members, and members of her kin group work together at different times of the year to build a birchbark house (*BH* 6–9, 221–22) and sweat lodge (*TPY* 54–55, *GOS* 117). In *COTL*, Ohkwa'ri works alone to build a coming-of-age lodge across the river from his village (43–52).

Building descriptions for an Inuit igloo (*COTS* 32–35), an Ojibwe birchbark house (*BH* 6–9), and a Mohawk coming-of-age shelter (*COTL* 43–52) follow.

Building a Traditional Inuit Igloo

The-man-with-no-eyebrows searches for the right kind of snow to build a new igloo for himself, his wife, and his new son. He pokes about the snowy landscape with a straightened piece of caribou antler and tests the snow for hardness, consistency, and depth. His new igloo first takes shape as a circle drawn with a stick in the snow. From within this circle he cuts and removes many blocks of snow with his special snow-knife, positions them at the edge of the circle, taps them into place, round and round, until the growing spiral of snow blocks form a domed wall closed at the top with a single block.

Building a Traditional Ojibwe Birchbark House

Omakayas's grandmother Nokomis, an experienced house builder, speaks directly to the old birch tree that will furnish its bark for a new spring house. She addresses the tree as Old Sister, expresses her need of bark for a new shelter, and deposits a fragrant offering of tobacco at the base of the tree to show her gratitude and respect. She strips bark from the tree, then sews the strips together into large mats of bark using her awl and thin bands of basswood thread.

Omakayas, her mother, and older sister Yellow Kettle all help their grandmother to build the family's new birchbark home. Omakayas's mother and sister construct a frame for the house using pliable willow poles. The new house is complete and ready to occupy when all the mats are fitted in place on the willow-pole frame.

Building a Traditional Mohawk Coming-of-Age Shelter

Ohkwa'ri builds a coming-of-age shelter for himself across the river from his clan's longhouse using simple tools and materials provided by the forest: maple saplings, elm bark, and strips of tough inner bark from a basswood tree. Before constructing his shelter, he gives thanks to a large maple tree and saplings for their sacrifice, addressing them as friends, then clears a patch of forest using his stone ax and knife, and digs 13 holes in the ground in a circle to receive his framing poles.

When his framing poles are set firmly in the ground, he bends each pole inward toward the others, crisscrossing them on top, and lashing them securely together with strips of basswood bark. The frame of his emerging shelter now resembles a turtle shell. Now to strengthen the frame, he adds thinner poles crosswise at intervals around the sides and leaves an opening, an open doorway, facing the river. After fastening his set of elm bark shingles to his arched frame, his coming-of-age shelter is complete.

Boat Building and Repair

Prominent individuals in *GOS* and *COTS* work together or alone to build a traditional Ojibwe family canoe or to build or repair a traditional Inuit kayak. In *GOS*, Omakayas helps her parents, grandmother, and Old Tallow to build a new birchbark canoe for family travel (67–74).

In *COTS*, Wolverine's father and father-in-law work together and Wolverine works alone to build personal kayaks for summer travel and hunting (75, 83, 107). Also in *COTS*, in preparation for his long journey home by sea from Marble Island, Wolverine repairs his own kayak using traditional Inuit materials and methods (131). He adds new lashings to the wooden frame and repairs all the holes in the sealskin covering using a bone needle and whale sinew.

In *WP*, Saxso comes upon a new birchbark canoe left upside down by the river and reflects on its construction (84). The building of a traditional Ojibwe birchbark canoe is described in detail in *GOS*.

Net Making

In *HTS*, on separate trips to the island across the lake from their cabin, Owl's mom continues to make a new fish net with her netting tools and line and finally dyes it with a special solution made with boiled pine cones (34, 50).

Tanning

Prominent individuals in three novels tan hides using traditional Indigenous methods and materials. In *COTS*, Wolverine's future mother-in-law and fiance tan a sealskin for a pair of new boots (102). In *GOS*, Omakayas helps her grandmother to tan hides. At one time Omakayas and her older sister help their grandmother to tan a deer hide that her grandmother plans to sell to the trader (58). At another time Omakayas helps her grandmother to tan a moose hide, helping her to scrape the hide while it is draped over a log, as shown in an illustration (93).

In *BH*, Omakayas helps her mother to tan a moose hide for new moccasins (14–15). Her mother has tanned the hide partially herself, having removed excess flesh and hair from each side of the hide, applied a special mixture of moose brains to the hide to soften it, and left the hide to soak overnight in water. Now Omakayas takes over. She stretches the hide as it dries using a special tool shown on page 36 and keeps the hide soft until the whole hide is dry.

Traditional Clothes and Clothing Accessories

Prominent individuals from five Indigenous Nations wear traditional clothes and clothing accessories and produce traditional moccasins or mitts for themselves or others. Clothing styles, clothing accessories, and traditional moccasin or mitt production reflect the traditions of Ojibwe, Inuit, Mohawk, Abenaki, and Choctaw peoples.

Articles of clothing are specifically identified in 12 novels (e.g., a leather jacket, a skirt, a loincloth). However, in two novels traditional clothing is simply referred to as tanned leather, deerskin, or buckskin clothes (*TPY* 21, 105, *SM* 26, 79).

Traditional Clothes

Traditional clothes are identified in seven novels. The clothes identified include leather dresses (*SM* 60, *WITD* 79), a woolen baby dress (*BH* 1), a long skirt (*LV* 76), a homemade blouse (*LV* 76), caribou-skin pants (*COTS* 104), loincloths (*WP* 23, *COTL* 77), and leggings (*WP* 23, *BH* 41).

Traditional Clothing Accessories

A fire-making pouch (*TPY* 7), a leather jacket (*BH* 73), jewelry, leather mittens, coats, footwear, and headwear are identified in 11 novels. Identified jewelry includes a braided rawhide bracelet (*SM* 60) and a turtle shell necklace (*SRC* 55). In two of three *Birchbark House* series novels traditional deer and moose hide mittens are identified (*BH* 74, 122, 194, 129) and the production of leather mittens and moccasins described (*GOS* 184–85, *BH* 130).

Identified coats include a caribou-skin coat (*COTS* 48, 104), a deerskin coat (*WP* 23), an inner caribou-skin coat (*COTS* 104), and favorite homemade coats made of home-tanned leather and fur (*TPY* 100, *BH* 114, 124).

Traditional ankle rubbers and moccasin lining made from rabbit fur are identified in two novels (*HTS* 26, *BH* 177). Traditional footwear identified in eight novels includes waterproof knee-high work boots with and without bearskin bottoms (*COTS* 103, 104) and various kinds of moccasins—from plain moccasins (*WIB* 20, *SM* 60, *WP* 23, *COTL* 64, *HTS* 117, 147, *BH* 22, 73, 122) to lined moccasins (*TPY* 105, *BH* 17) to knee-high moccasins (*TPY*

21). Identified headwear includes leather hoods (*BH* 74), a tam (*LV* 76), a beaver-skin cap (*LV* 60), and a white fur trapper's hat (*MT* 75).

Blankets and Blanket Making

Traditional blankets are identified in three novels. Traditional rabbit blankets are identified in *TPY* (102) and *GOS* (99), and a traditional star quilt and buffalo robe are identified in *LLM* (27, 71). The traditional Ojibwe method for making rabbit blankets is described briefly in *GOS* (99), and in *LLM* a detailed description of traditional Lakota quilt making is provided by Lori's grandmother, a skilled Lakota quilter (27–31).

Mats and Baskets

Traditional mats and baskets are identified in five novels. The traditional Ojibwe method for making pukwe mats is described briefly in *GOS* (31). Traditional Abenaki, Ojibwe, and Mohawk baskets, identified in three novels, are made from ash tree fibers (*MTTT* 5–6, 14), elm bark (*COTL* 10), and birch bark (*LV* 41).

Details about the process of obtaining ash tree fibers for traditional Abenaki baskets are provided in *MTTT*, and the specific uses of traditional Mohawk and Ojibwe baskets are identified in *COTL* and *LV*. The traditional elm bark basket in *COTL* holds fresh strawberries recently collected by Ohkwa'ri's sister, and the traditional birchbark basket in *LV* holds two rabbits recently cleaned and prepared for cooking by Ray's grandmother.

Wood Carving

Prominent individuals in four novels engage in wood carving with knives or chisels to produce various household and sculpted objects with or without ornamentation, and Saxso in *WP* spots the figure of a leaping salmon carved in relief on the side of a birchbark canoe (84). Ten-year-old Owl in *HTS* has become quite skilled at carving spindles out of cedar wood, which her mother uses for making fish nets. Each spindle is roughly five inches long, an inch wide, and has a long pointed tongue in the middle. Owl carves each spindle first, then sands it. Each spindle holds a good amount of fishing twine.

Will's father in *WG* and Ohkwa'ri's uncle in *COTL* are both experienced and dedicated wood carvers. Will's father carves mainly in the Sto:lo and West Coast Native traditions, and produces plain and decorative wooden objects such as bowls, spoons, plates, figurines, family crests, and ceremonial masks. Ohkwa'ri's uncle Big Tree carves in the Mohawk tradition, produces special wooden objects for ceremonial purposes and special events, and is widely revered for his public carvings.

During the Strawberry Moon, Big Tree continues to carve the interior of a special coming-of-age cup for his nephew Ohkwa'ri made from the hard and durable wood of a maple tree. This new cup will replace the chipped cup hanging from Ohkwa'ri's belt, a boy's cup made from a soft piece of bass-wood. Ohkwa'ri aims to be a skilled carver like his uncle one day. He watches his uncle one night expanding the bowl of the new cup. His uncle adds a hot coal to the interior of the cup, blows on the coal, moves the coal around, then uses a sharp stone to clean the burned wood from the bowl.

Ornamentation

Prominent individuals in seven novels identify, describe, or engage in dis-tinctive Indigenous ornamentation practices including beadwork, quillwork, tattooing, and embroidery.

Beadwork and Quillwork

In *WG*, Will and his cousin Sarah both do beadwork. Will occasionally beads with female family members and Sarah regularly produces beaded things like barrettes, bags, and vamps for moccasins (14, 32). In *HTS*, Owl's mom works at beading at home in the fall and while camping out during the sum-mer (46, 66). In *WIB*, Carrie makes a pair of beaded booties for a new baby in the family (69).

In *BH,* Omakayas describes in varying degrees of detail a beaded woolen case used by her mother for sewing (17), a beaded pouch (22), a beaded traveling bag (124–26), a beaded dress (22), beaded summer and winter moccasins (48, 129), a beaded cradleboard wrapping (43), and a beaded pipe (75). In *BH* and *GOS*, Omakayas notes the tight rows of beads in her sister's and mother's beadwork designs (*BH* 10, 48) and the notable ornamentation of a beaded vest and bandolier bag with the traditional beadwork elements of green vines, colorful flowers, and an elegant background of expensive white glass beads (*GOS* 200–202, *BH* 124–26).

Omakayas's grandmother Nokomis is uniquely skilled at quillwork. Omakayas acknowledges her grandmother's skill to ornament such things as traveling bags and dance fans using dyed porcupine quills (*BH* 124, 127). Omakayas also notes at the tail-end of winter, while seated by the fireside with her grandmother, that Nokomis often engages in quillwork while sharing traditional stories with her grandchildren (171).

Tattooing and Embroidery Work

Traditional tattoo designs, traditional tattooing practices, and an embroidered bunting bag with traditional emblems are described briefly or in detail in three novels. In *WP*, Saxso spots traditional tattoo designs on the chest and back of an old man (23). These designs include a big snake, a flying bird, stars, and symbols representing the four directions. In *COTL*, Ohkwa'ri recalls the personal experience of a local boy who received his unflattering new name as the result of a poorly articulated tattoo (75–77).

In *WIB*, Carrie's grandmother shows Carrie an embroidered bunting bag, a gift for her grandmother's new great-grandchild made by Carrie's sister (70). The bunting bag sports the traditional images of a wolf and bear rendered in embroidery thread.

Toy Making

Traditional Indigenous toys are made by prominent individuals in two novels. In *GOS*, Deydey makes traditional Ojibwe toys for his youngest two children: a toy cradleboard for Omakayas and a toy rattle for her baby brother (165). In *WIB*, with expert guidance from her sister, Carrie uses traditional Mohawk materials and methods to make her first corn husk doll (78–79).

SET 7.6 TRADITIONAL IMPLEMENTS AND MATERIALS

Traditional Implements

Traditional Indigenous implements are identified and described in varying degrees of detail in eight novels. For the purposes of this book, an implement is defined as a tool, utensil, or other piece of equipment used in doing work.[1] As shown in table 6.1, a variety of implements are used by individuals in eight novels to access water, eat, make fire, and more. These implements range from ice chisels and spoons to strikers, lamps, awls, and axes.

Traditional Weapons

Traditional Indigenous weapons used for hunting and defense are identified in nine novels. These weapons include a harpoon (*COTS* 107), a deer-bone knife (*SRC* 49), spears (*LLM* 81, *COTS* 107, *DP* 67), slingshots (*LV* 210, *HTS* 11, *SW* 170), a fighting club (*COTL* 16), a fighting knife (*WP* 128), a tomahawk (*WP* 128), and arrowheads (*LLM* 81).

Table 6.1. Traditional implements identified in eight novels

Implement	Use	Novel & Page
ice chisel	accessing lake water	*SW* 235, *BH* 122
beading hoops	beading	*GOS* 202
knife, ulu	cutting	*BH* 7, *COTS* 89
wooden water cup	drinking	*COTL* 31
wooden bowl	eating	*TPY* 169
wooden spoon	eating	*TPY* 169
horn spoon	eating	*LLM* 81
blowpipe	fire stoking	*COTL* 31
flint	fire-making	*TPY* 7, *COTS* 126
striker	fire-making	*TPY* 7
horn hoe	gardening	*BH* 56
digging tool	gardening	*GOS* 28
seal-oil lamp	indoor lighting	*COTS* 127
awl	sewing	*TPY* 170
needle	sewing	*COTS* 127
fleshing tool	tanning	*TPY* 148
hide scraper	tanning	*BH* 68
rice knockers	wild rice harvesting	*GOS* 78
ax	wood crafting	*LV* 40, *BH* 122

Traditional Materials

Traditional Indigenous materials are identified and described in varying degrees of detail in seven novels. A comprehensive list of these materials and their uses is shown in table 6.2. Traditional Indigenous materials are provided by plant and animal sources in local environments. These natural materials are obtained from trees (saplings, branches, bark, wood chips, roots), the floor of old forests (moss, lichen), wetlands (cotton grass), large-game animals (sinew, hide, brains, bones), seals (skin), bears (claws, teeth), and various small-game animals and birds (fur, claws).

SET 7.7 TRADITIONAL FOODS, DRINKS, AND MEDICINES

Traditional Foods

Traditional Indigenous foods are identified in over half of the novels explored in this book, and many of these foods, derived from local plant and animal resources, were previously identified in Set 7.2. Additional traditional foods are identified below in six groups. The sixth group includes traditional foods that are not readily located in the other five groups.

Table 6.2. Traditional materials used in seven novels

Material	Use	Novel & Page
sinew	beading	*BH* 127
	making rabbit snares	*TPY* 12
	making ceremonial outfits	*WG* 14
	stitching together pieces of moose hide	*MT* 49
twining root	catching eagles	*TPY* 51
sumac branch	making a blowpipe	*COTL* 30
rabbit fur	making blankets	*BH* 121
sealskin	making boots	*COTS* 103
elm bark	making canoes	*COTL* 7
birchbark	making canoes	*COTL* 7
bear claws	making ceremonial outfits	*WG* 14
eagle claws	making ceremonial outfits	*WG* 14
grouse claws	making ceremonial outfits	*WG* 14
bear teeth	making ceremonial outfits	*WG* 14
leather	making ceremonial outfits	*WG* 14
maple saplings	making lodge poles	*COTL* 43
lichen	making mattresses	*COTS* 127
moss	making mattresses	*COTS* 127
moose hide	making moccasins	*SM* 75
	making tarps, blankets, ponchos	*MT* 49
deer bones	making necklaces	*WG* 14
moose bone	making pegs and chisels	*MT* 49
basswood twine	making rabbit snares	*TYP* 101
willow bark	making smoke racks	*LV* 208
hickory wood	making Tekwaarathon sticks	*COTL* 105
basswood	making water cups	*COTL* 31
moss	portaging	*TPY* 19
moose brains	tanning	*BH* 14
dried moss, cotton grass	oil lamp wicking	*COTL* 127

Fresh, Boiled, Fried, Roasted, Dried, Smoked, and Powdered Meat

Meat obtained from large- and small-game animals, seals, freshwater fish, and several species of birds are staple foods in 11 novels. Animals whose meat contributes substantially to traditional Ojibwe, Choctaw, Narragansett, and Inuit diets include deer (*TPY* 103, *SRC* 303, *WITD* xii, *WP* 108), muskrats (*HTS* 184), rabbits (*TPY* 40, *COTS* 46, *LV* 39, *HTS* 24, *SW* 135, *BH* 145), seals (*COTS* 127), and squirrels (*SRC* 54).

In many of these novels meat is served in a variety of ways: boiled, fried, roasted, dried, smoked, or powdered. Meat servings such as these include boiled meat (*GOS* 3), fried fish (*HTS* 119), fried rabbit meat (*LV* 33), roasted partridge (*SW* 120), roasted blackbirds (*BH* 60), roasted rabbits (*LV* 33, *HTS*

184, *SW* 140), dried meat (*TPY* 80, *MT* 184, *BH* 162), buffalo jerky (*LLM* 81), caribou jerky (*COTS* 127), dried fish (*BH* 196), smoked deer meat (*COTL* 79), and powdered fish (*BH* 196).

Soup, Broth, and Stew

Meat obtained from local environments is also used to produce soups, broths, or stews. Traditional Ojibwe, Choctaw, and Inuit soup, broth, and stew dishes include deer meat soup (*TPY* 29, *GOS* 3), fish soup (*GOS* 36), rabbit soup (*BH* 145), fish broth (*BH* 194), moose stew (*BH* 12), fish stew (*TPY* 48, *SW* 157), stewed rabbits (*LV* 33), and partridge stew (*HTS* 46). In *COTS*, a special broth is produced from boiled seal meat and roots (127).

Corn and caribou bones are used traditionally by Choctaw and Inuit peoples to produce special soups. Pashofa corn soup is a traditional soup identified in *SRC* (303), and caribou bone soup is a traditional soup identified in *COTS* (86).

Baking Powder Breads, Puddings, and Dumplings

Different types of Indigenous breads, dumplings, and puddings are identified as traditional foods in nine novels. Bannock, a type of Indigenous bread risen with baking powder, is identified as a traditional food in *TPY* (29), *WG* (23), *LV* (2), *HTS* (14), *BH* (88), and *GOS* (3). Bannock wound around a stick and roasted over an open fire, fried bannock, and raisin bannock are all traditional Ojibwe foods identified in *SW* (131), *SW* (58), and *HTS* (114).

Other types of Indigenous breads are identified in five novels. These breads are traditional Mohawk, Choctaw, and Lakota breads that include baked cornbread (*WIB* 66), boiled cornbread (*SRC* 160), banaha bread (*SRC* 303), pumpkin bread (*SRC* 54), and fry [*sic*] bread (*LLM* 81). Blackberry pudding is another traditional Choctaw food (*SRC* 168), and dumplings are identified as a traditional Mohawk and Ojibwe food in *WIB* (67) and *LV* (33).

Fruit, Vegetables, Legumes, Rice, Nuts, and Roots

A variety of wild berries picked locally or from traditional locations accessible by traditional land or water routes are identified in 10 novels. Wild berries identified as traditional Choctaw, Mohawk, Abenaki, Ojibwe, and Sto: lo foods include strawberries (*TPY* 33, *COTL* 9), blackberries (*SRC* 54, *COTL* 65, *WP* 107), blueberries (*WG* 5, *LV* 11, *WP* 107, *HTS* 19, *BH* 60), saskatoon berries (*WG* 12), chokecherries (*LLM* 21), highbush cranberries (*TPY* 103), lowbush cranberries (*LV* 79, also called moss berries), and salmon berries (*WG* 12).

A variety of vegetables, legumes, rice, nuts, and roots grown or collected locally are identified as traditional Indigenous foods in six novels. Vegetables identified in these novels include corn (*TPY* 103, *HR* 10, *SRC* 56, *COTL* 22, *BH* 60), peppers (*HR* 10), squash (*TPY* 103, *HR* 10, *COTL* 22), wild carrots (*LV* 89), and wild onions (*SRC* 303, *BH* 60). Beans, wild rice, acorns, hazelnuts, arrowroot roots, and cattail roots are identified as traditional Abenaki, Mohawk, and Ojibwe foods in *HR* (10), *COTL* (22), *TPY* (89, 108), *BH* (176), and *WP* (108).

Fats and Sweets

Fats and sweets identified as traditional Ojibwe, Sto: lo, Mohawk, and Abenaki foods are identified in six novels. Traditional fats include bone marrow (*TPY* 174, *BH* 230) and candlefish grease (*WG* 5). Traditional sweets include maple sugar (*TPY* 75, *HR* 38, *BH* 24) and maple syrup (*COTL* 53, *BH* 17, *GOS* 3).

Other Traditional Foods

Other traditional Ojibwe, Choctaw, Abenaki, and Mohawk foods include (plain) corn pashofa (*SRC* 54), pemmican (*TPY* 49, *LV* 89, *COTL* 79, *HTS* 168), moose nose (*LV* 89), pumpkin flowers (*BH* 196), inner pine tree bark (*WP* 107), and lichen (*TPY* 181).

Traditional Drinks

Traditional Indigenous drinks are identified in six novels. All but one drink— a special strawberry drink produced during the Strawberry Thanksgiving Festival (*COTL* 12)—are identified as teas: wintergreen tea (*BH* 60), Labrador or swamp tea (*LV* 94, *BH* 145), balsam tea (*TPY* 108), corn-hair tea (*WIB* 79), and sassafras root tea (*SRC* 198). These teas are typically served hot.

Traditional Medicines

Specific plants, flowers, trees, and mushrooms and several unnamed trees and plants, harvested locally and used for medicinal purposes wet or dry, are identified in five novels. In *MTTT*, a medicinal tea brewed with needles obtained from white pine trees is used to treat deep hacking coughs (7), and mullein leaves are used for poultices (102). In *COTL*, bloodroot flowers are used for dressing cuts and wounds (56).

The medicinal properties and traditional uses of puffball mushrooms by Abenaki and Ojibwe peoples are identified in *WP* and *GOS*. In both novels, puffball mushrooms are used medicinally to stop bleeding and heal cuts, sores, rashes, and scrapes (*WP* 49, *GOS* 101). In *GOS*, in the fall, Omakayas scouts about for these specific mushrooms with her grandmother in the nearby forest, notes the silky powders exuded by these mushrooms when squeezed, and describes several ways this powder helped to heal her father and baby brother (101).

In all five novels, the sources of some traditional medicines are not disclosed. In *GOS*, the bark obtained from an unidentified local tree is used to brew a special tea that strengthens the blood (215); and in *MTTT*, an unidentified plant leaf is used for treating burns (120). Finally, several unnamed plants, used for medicinal purposes, are noted in *LV* (224), *COTL* (54), and *BH* (9, 103, 158).

Food Preparation

Traditional Indigenous methods of preparing animals, fish, and birds are identified and described in varying degrees of detail in seven novels. Large and small animals and whales are butchered (*COTS* 86, *HTS* 189, *SW* 155) and skinned (*TPY* 42, *COTS* 86, *SW* 113). Fish are scaled (*LV* 80, *HTS* 38) and deboned (*GOS* 24). Blackbirds and ducks are plucked (*BH* 60) and singed (*SW* 155).

Traditional Indigenous foods including fish and animal meat, maple syrup, and corn are dried (*COTS* 86, *BH* 99, *GOS* 33), pounded (*BH* 99); roasted, smoked, or boiled slowly over an open fire (*TPY* 18, 165, *SW* 155, 156, 160). Animals and fish are eviscerated (*LV* 80, *HTS* 38, *SW* 155, *BH* 99, *GOS* 34). The careful smoking of wild rice on woven mats is described in detail in *BH* (165).

Food Storage

Traditional Indigenous food storage methods are identified in six novels. Food is cached during the winter (*TPY* 45, *COTS* 84, *BH* 100), stored temporarily in wooden food boxes (*SW* 129, *HTS* 13), or stored in a birchbark container for shorter or longer intervals of time (*GOS* 17). Pemmican—a favorite Ojibwe traveling food made from powdered deer meat, berries, and fat—is stored in special leather pouches (*TPY* 49).

NOTE

1. *American Heritage Dictionary*, s.v. "implement (n.)," accessed February 4, 2023, https://www.ahdictionary.com/implement.

Chapter 7

Group C

Language Use, Stories, and Storytelling

CHAPTER OVERVIEW

Indigenizing fictional world features in Group C and the Category of Language Use, Stories, and Storytelling are examined in this chapter. Two sets of Category 8 features are examined. In all, 15 indigenizing features are identified, described, and illustrated in this chapter.

8. Language Use, Storytelling, and Stories
    8.1 Language use: ancestral language, names and naming
    8.2 Storytelling, stories, and writing: storytelling time, art of storytelling, stories about the Creator, stories about culture heroes, stories about legendary individuals, mythical stories, stories about animal tricksters, evil being stories, eagle stories, personal stories, family stories, widelycirculated stories of contemporary renown, Indigenous writing

8. LANGUAGE USE, STORYTELLING, AND STORIES

The use of an Indigenous language by prominent individuals or whole communities of Indigenous peoples for daily communication, storytelling, special events, personal names, or other purposes is a distinguishing feature of Indigenized fictional worlds.

SET 8.1 LANGUAGE USE

Ancestral Language

Indigenous languages are used by prominent individuals in 20 novels. Inuktitut, Mohawk, and Ojibwe are used exclusively in *COTS*, *COTL*, and all three *Birchbark House* series novels. Ojibwe, Abenaki, and Choctaw are used extensively in *HTS*, *LV*, *WP*, *NMNN*, and *SRC*. Ojibwe and Navajo are used intermittently in *SW* and all three *Danny Blackgoat* series novels. Choctaw, Narragansett, Ojibwe, Cree, Lakota, and Abenaki are identified as living languages in *NN*, *WITD*, *MT*, *LLM*, and *MTTT*.

The months of the year appear both in Lakota and English in the fore matter of *LLM*. A glossary of Ojibwe words appears in each novel in the *Birchbark House* series. Examples of glossed words from the *Birchbark House* novels include the following:

biboon	winter
makuk	container
manomin	wild rice
bizindaan	listen
weyass	meat
zagimeg	mosquitoes
aadizookaan	traditional story
binesi	thunderbird
jeemaan	canoe
mashkiki	medicine
migiziins	eagle
tikinagun	cradleboard

Readers will quickly infer that all fictional world individuals in *COTS*, *COTL*, and the three *Birchbark House* series novels are communicating exclusively with each other in an Indigenous language—Inuktitut, Mohawk, or Ojibwe. The appearance of Indigenous words is most prevalent in *COTS*. Inuktitut words appear in all 23 chapters in the novel and on almost every page. Inuktitut words are given for ancestral locations, ancestral beings, everyday objects and actions, animals, games, and more.

An Indigenous language is the first language of eight prominent young people. These eight individuals include Wolverine (Inuktitut, *COTS*), Omakayas (Ojibwe, *BH*, *TPY*, *GOS*), twin siblings Ohkaw'ri and Otsi:stia (Mohawk, *COTL*), Owl (Ojibwe, *HTS*), Martha Tom (Choctaw, *SRC*), Saxso (Abenaki, *WP*), Louis Nolette (Abenaki, *MTTT*), and Danny Blackgoat (*DBNP*, *DBRRTF*, *DBDP*)

Names and Naming

Individuals in 11 novels have Shawnee, Abenaki, Choctaw, Ojibwe, Mohawk, or Inuktitut names, and details about the origins of two Inuktitut names beyond mere English translations is provided in *COTS*.

> *Shawnee and Abenaki names in DP and WP*: Quoshtoki (waterfall) (*DP*); Two Sticks, Beaver's Tail, The Worrier, Samadagwis, Awasos, Obomsawin (*WP*). *Choctaw names in NN and SRC*: No Name, Whispering Wind, Cherokee Johnny (*NN*); Squirrel Man (Funi Man), Panther Boy (Koi Losa), Shonti, Blue Doe (*SRC*).
>
> *Ojibwe names in BH, TPY, GOS*: Little Frog (Omakayas), Ice (Mikwam), Old Tallow, Fishtail, Little Thunder (Animikiins), Baby Wildcat (Bizheens), Yellow Kettle, Pinch, Chickadee, Two Strike Girl, Auntie Muskrat, Twilight, Little Bee (Amoosens), Ten Snow, Leading Thunder Woman (Ogimabineskiwe), Red Thunder (Miskobines), Angry Boy. Ojibwe name in *HTS*: The Owl. Ojibwe names in *MT*: Miigwans (Miig), Tree, Zheegwon, Wab, Chi-boy, Slopper.
>
> *Mohawk names in COTL*: Ohkwa'ri, Grabber, Greasy Hair, Eats Like a Bear, The Flower (Otsi:stia), Herons Flying, She Opens the Sky, The One Who Has Two Ideas (Dagaheo'ga), Big Tree, Falls a Lot, Hand Talker, Little Fox, Two Claws, Thunder's Voice, Wide Awake, Watches Everything, Red Ducks, Quick Eyes, Bear's Son, Great Bear (Ktsiwassos).
>
> *Inuktitut names in COTS*: The-man-with-no-eyebrows (Qabluttuq), Can't-see, Wolverine (Qavvik), Auk, Paaliaq, Breath (Anirniq), Little-loved-one (Kuluk), Paammakuluk. Inuktitut naming in *COTS*. The-man-with-no-eyebrows and his son Wolverine are both named after respected forbears, a traditional Inuit naming practice. In chapter 1, The-man-with-no-eyebrows supposes that the first The-man-with-no-eyebrows, who lived and died long ago, had faint eyebrows or none at all and received his name as a nickname. At some point in his life long ago, this first The-man-with-no-eyebrows must have distinguished himself in some way, and his name was formalized and passed down through the generations. Wolverine is named after his paternal grandfather (5–6).

SET 8.2 STORYTELLING, STORIES, AND WRITING

Prominent individuals in 14 novels recognize the importance of storytelling in their lives, identify specific seasons of the year as storytelling seasons, describe the artistry of particular storytellers in the community, identify specific forms of writing as Indigenous writing, recount personal experiences or the experience of an ancestor, or share a traditional Indigenous story with one or more people. Traditional stories appear in all 14 novels. These stories focus on the Creator, culture heroes, legendary individuals, an extraordinary achievement by a living person, animal tricksters, evil beings, or eagles.

In *TPY*, Omakayas explicitly recognizes the importance of stories for herself and her family members. In chapter 12 during the Wiindigoo Moon, she reminds herself of the life-sustaining importance of stories during winter, at other times of the year, and throughout the life cycle. Her grandmother told stories to raise people's spirits during difficult times. She also told stories for instructional purposes and healing (122).

Storytelling Time

As noted in the historical novels *BH* (171), *TPY* (122), and *COTL* (19, 20, 54, 58–59), stories focusing on personal experiences from the recent or distant past could be shared freely during any season of the year by Ojibwe and Mohawk peoples, but sacred creation stories, mythical stories, stories about legendary individuals, and trickster stories were only shared during the winter.

The Art of Storytelling

In *WG* chapter 1, Will reflects on the artful way Sto: loh women tell stories (8). While lying in bed one night, with moonlight streaming through his window, Will pictures three familiar Sto: loh women—his mother, grandmother, and aunt—seated at a table, sharing stories. He is there too, somewhere in the background, listening secretly to the women's stories and conversation.

Lying there in the moonlight, sleepy but awake, Will notes that Sto: loh women tell stories in a particular way. They begin with the end of a story first, and if the ending arouses interest, they tell that story through to the end, detail by detail. That kitchen scene plays out quickly in Will's head—those three familiar women at a table—his aunt telling a story in a customary way, beginning with an ending, capturing her listeners' interest and attention, telling the story artfully.

Stories About the Creator

Stories about the Creator appear in two novels. In *COTL*, Otsi:stia recalls the Mohawk story of how medicines were given to Bear Clan women by the

Creator (54–57). In *WP*, Saxso recalls the Abenaki story about changes in water flow brought about by the Creator (96).

Stories About Culture Heroes

Some traditional stories focus on the activities of a culture hero, a mystical being partly supernatural and partly human, that typifies, embodies, preserves, and transmits distinctive features of a culture. According to the *Dictionary of Native American Mythology* (Gill and Sullivan 1992), most culture heroes have proper names, possess superhuman powers, are frequently on the move, and commonly appear in creation stories.

Culture heroes are identified in four novels: Iktomi (Lakota) in *LLM*, Gluskabe (Abenaki) in *WP*, and Nanabozho (Anishinabe) in *BH* and *TPY*. No specific stories about Iktomi are shared in *LLM*, but two stories each are shared about Gluskabe and Nanabozho in the other novels.

The stories about Gluskabe in *WP* are both transformational stories. In one story Gluskabe transforms the land by defeating a giant beaver (10); and in the other story, he transforms skunk grass into sweet grass (58). The stories about Nanabozho in *BH* and *TPY* are transformational and trickster stories respectively. In *BH*, Nanabozho remakes the earth with Muskrat's help (172–75); and in *TPY,* he endeavors to outwit a buffalo encountered during his travels (130–31).

The Lakota Culture Hero Iktomi

Iktomi (the Spider) is a popular character in the sacred stories of the Sioux Nation, a confederacy of seven councils and their respective communities that includes the Lakota people. According to Powers (1975), the genre of sacred stories focuses on the activities and antics of supernatural beings like Iktomi whose transformative powers allow them to change shape and appear in diverse forms. In many sacred Siouan stories, the character of Iktomi appears in the form of a handsome man, who is constantly on the go, seeking out animals and pranking them.

Time, space, and language were all created by Iktomi, and Iktomi was responsible for naming all things and giving animals their distinctive colors and shapes. Mischievous, deceptive, reckless, and self-absorbed, Iktomi frequently violates Siouan social norms and treats his body irreverently or like a toy.

The Abenaki Culture Hero Gluskabe

According to Day (1976), more is known about the culture hero Gluskap (Gluskabe) from Micmac (i.e., Mi'kmaq) and Malecite (i.e., Maliseet) sources than from Abenaki sources. As all three nations are members of the Wabanaki Confederacy and are similar culturally and linguistically, details about the character of Gluskap found in Micmac and Malecite stories will likely reflect to some degree Abenaki understandings about Gluskabe.

In the storytelling traditions of Micmac and Malecite peoples, Gluskap (Glooscap) was a benevolent superhuman being, who appeared one day in a stone boat with his mother or grandmother, and cared a great deal about people. Gluskap was formed a long time ago by the Creator, who shaped him from earth, gave him a human form, breathed life into him, and gave him supernatural powers. Gluskap used his powers to transform the land and make it more habitable for people.

In 1869, a Micmac man, Stephen Hood, reported to Rand (1893) that Glooscap was a sacred being, wise, thoughtful, and good, who befriended the Micmac people, guided them, and taught them important new things. He taught them about the arts, stars, and new techniques for hunting, fishing, harvesting food, and curing illnesses. Eventually he settled far in the west in a beautiful location with two mighty personages, Kahkw (Earthquake) and Koolpujot (No bones).

The Anishinabe Culture Hero Nanabozho

Johnston (1996) identifies Nanabozho's (Nana'b'oozoo) mother as Winonah, a human being, and his father as Ae-pungishimook, a supernatural being. Nanabozho was raised by his maternal grandmother and never knew his parents: his mother Winonah died in childbirth and his father had already abandoned his pregnant wife and two sons before Nanabozho was born. As a newborn, newly arrived in the world, Nanabozho astonished his grandmother by introducing himself by name, but in all other respects, his childhood and adolescent years were quite unremarkable.

For the longest time, Nanabozho's grandmother withheld the truth from him about his parents, but when he turned 20, she spoke candidly to him about his mother and his father's neglect. Blaming his father for his mother's premature death and the many hardships he himself experienced growing up as an orphan, Nanabozho decided to punish his father, declared war on him privately, held a traditional war ceremony in his village, filled his quiver with fine arrows, and set out west for the land of the spirits.

In one story about the Anishinabe culture hero Nanabozho, the further he traveled west as a young man of 20, the more fearful he became about the outcome of going to war with a supernatural being like his father. Such beings were incredibly powerful, and the further he traveled from his village, the more convinced he became that in a war with a supernatural being, he would likely end up dead. So he wisely changed course and did not return home for many years.

Nanabozho and Muskrat Make an Earth

This transformational story about the earth, the Ojibwe cultural hero Nanabozho, and a muskrat unfolds in four parts.

Part 1. Rain fell continuously for many days in the past and very quickly covered the land. Nanabozho escaped the rising flood waters first by climbing a hill, then by climbing a tall pine tree that stretched itself upward four times at Nanabozho's command to prevent him from drowning. The rain continued for some time with Nanabozho clinging to the top of the tree, then stopped. But at that point the flood waters had already reached Nanabozho's chin.

Part 2. Still clinging to the submerged tree, with only his head above water, Nanabozho looked around for a quick escape from his predicament and spotted three animals playing close to him in the water—Otter, Beaver, and Muskrat. He asked the first two animals in turn to fetch a handful of earth from the submerged ground below for him to remake the world. Each animal set out, lost his breath, and drowned.

Part 3. One animal remained, the smallest and weakest of the three. Nanabozho doubted that this last animal, Muskrat, could reach the ground below and return with a handful of earth, which the others, both larger and stronger than Muskrat, had failed to do, but he let Muskrat try. Muskrat drowned too. But when his lifeless body surfaced and Nanabozho examined it, he found bits of earth in Muskrat's paws and mouth.

Part 4. Nanabozho revived the three animals, beginning with Muskrat, placed each bit of earth in his hand, dried it in the sunlight, and tossed it in the water. A little island formed from these scattered bits of earth, and Nanabozho used new earth from this island to enlarge it and replenish it with animals.

Stories About Legendary Individuals

The online *Oxford English Dictionary* defines a legend as a traditional story sometimes popularly regarded as historical but not authenticated.[1] In scholarly use legend is distinguished from myth as typically involving (potentially) historical figures acting within an earthly environment, though supernatural elements are frequently present.

In this book, a story is designated as a legend if (i) a named person, believed to have existed at some point in the past, is both subject and theme and remains so for the full duration of the story, beginning to end, and if (ii) this person's name makes sense in the story's title (e.g., "The Legend of No Name," "The Legend of Bear Girl").

Stories about legendary individuals are shared in four novels. These legendary individuals include Chekabesh (*LV*), Bear Girl (*TPY*), Kiviuq (*COTS*), and No Name (*NN*).

Chekabesh (LV 86)

Shortly after bedtime on the night of her arrival at her grandmother's cabin, Ray is summoned outside by her grandmother's old friend Joshua to see the moon rising above the treetops. The moon is clearly visible in the night sky, completely round and remarkably large. The full moon reminds Joshua of the legendary story of Chekabesh who was seized by the moon, fetching water one night, and trapped there forever. According to Joshua the story teaches children that careless actions cannot be undone.

A longer though still fairly brief version of the story of Chekabesh (Chekadum), recounted below, appears in Stevens's (1971) collection of sacred legends told by the Sandy Lake Nation in Ontario. The version of this story unfolds in three parts.

Part 1. An old woman took charge of a young boy whom she had never seen before, named the boy Chekabesh (Chekadum) for his cheerful disposition, and raised the boy as her son. As a young man, her adopted son Chekabesh proved to be an able hunter and provided well for the old woman and himself. But in time, the old woman began to have nightmares as foretold by the stranger who left the young boy in her care. An alarmingly bright moon appeared repeatedly in the old woman's dreams and made her fearful about the future.

Part 2. Troubled by her recent dreams, the old woman warned her son, now a young man, not to look at the moon when coming and going by moonlight. But one night in early winter, the young man set off to fetch water with his dipper and pail and was so enchanted by the moon and its dazzling light that he grew careless, forgot the old woman's warning, looked up at the luminous moon, and stared at it senselessly.

The old woman waited patiently for her son to return that night, but as time wore on, his continuing absence filled her with dread. She set off after him, desperate to bring him home, tracking him through the snow, moving swiftly through the luminous night. Then suddenly she stopped. Her son's footprints and trail had suddenly vanished.

Part 3. The old woman looked around, looked up, and spotted her son on the moon, standing there lifelessly, trapped there forever with his dipper and pail.

Bear Girl (TPY 122–128)

The story of Bear Girl happened long ago and unfolds in four parts.

Part 1. Bear Girl was the youngest of three daughters whose parents were old and poor. Unlike her parents and sisters, Bear Girl was an actual bear. She was covered with fur and had long sharp teeth. Bear Girl was a very good daughter, neither vain nor selfish like her sisters, and her parents loved her very much. They called her Makoons (Little Bear).

Part 2. As time went on and all three daughters matured, the two older sisters got tired of being single, abandoned their parents and family home, and set out for a distant village, seeking husbands for themselves. Bear Girl followed them three times; and each time her sisters took her home and took stronger action to prevent her from pursuing them. First they tied her tightly to a clump of tough-rooted rushes, then to a great rock, then to a tree. They were ashamed of Bear Girl's appearance and didn't want their sister spoiling their marriage plans.

Part 3. None of the constraints imposed on Bear Girl by her sisters worked, and in her fourth encounter with them at the edge of a dangerous river, she proved herself to be a valuable companion, helped her sisters to cross the river safely, then joined her sisters on their journey. Later that night, Bear Girl proved her worth again as a travel companion when she saved her sisters from an evil woman who sought to kill them.

The evil woman lived en route to the village where Bear Girl's sisters hoped to find husbands. She invited the travelers to spend the night in her lodge, then tried to kill them with food and earrings. Bear Girl outwitted the evil woman, and fled from the lodge with her sisters. But in the evil woman's rage at being outwitted by the sisters, she plucked the moon and sun from the sky and locked them up in her lodge.

Part 4. Later that night, guided only by starlight, the three sisters arrived at the distant village and found the villagers wildly distressed about the darkness. After a quick consultation with Bear Girl and her sisters, the village chief charged Bear Girl with the task of recovering the moon and sun and restoring them to the sky, promising to reward her with husbands for her sisters. But to Bear Girl's great surprise, having completed her task successfully, not only were her sisters given husbands, but she too was given a husband, the chief's youngest and handsomest son.

Bear Girl's marriage did not go well. Her new husband resented being married to a bear. He ignored his new wife and made her sleep on the floor. Finally Bear Girl gave up on her marriage and entreated her husband to throw her in the fire, which he did. Bear Girl's sisters loved her now, reached out to save her, but the flames were too hot, and they failed. Later when the flames died down, all at once a beautiful young woman rose from the glowing coals, Bear Girl now human.

Bear Girl rejected the desperate pleading of her husband to take him back. She gave her sisters a goodbye and returned home to take care of their old parents.

Kiviuq (COTS 63–73, 130)

In chapter 12, Breath's grandmother sits close to her young granddaughter and playmate Wolverine on her bed and tells them a magical story about the first Inuit person and likely the last—the great Kiviuq, the greatest man who ever lived—who is still alive but extremely old. She prefaces her story about Kiviuq by telling them about an orphan boy whose new sealskin suit makes him a powerful swimmer, transports him far out to sea, and enables him to take his revenge on a group of boys who constantly torment him.

Kiviuq is among the boys who spot the seal-boy swimming near shore, mistake the boy for a seal, and pursue him in kayaks. The seal-boy whips up the sea with a special song, and all the boys drown except Kiviuq. Kiviuq is a very strong boy and agilely turns himself and his kayak upright whenever a wave knocks him over. The story of the great Kiviuq starts here and unfolds in two main parts.

Part 1. For many days and nights, traveling many miles alone, Kiviuq paddled his kayak until the wind eventually weakened and the sea grew calm. Overcome by exhaustion, he leaned against his paddle and fell asleep. He woke from a long sleep, rested but lost. Not a trace of land appeared in the distance, just water, endless stretches of sea.

Part 2. Kiviuq stayed calm, leaned on his paddle, and swept the horizon for land. Then a small bird, a snow bunting, lighted on his kayak, attracted by the feather on the back of his coat. The bird flew up three times after that in three different directions, and each time Kiviuq followed the bird. After two false sightings of land, Kiviuq finally reached land, a strange land no one had seen before.

No Name (NN 48–76)

In chapters 8–11, a high school history teacher and good friend of Bobby's father shares a long story with Bobby about the legendary Choctaw individual called No Name. The story unfolds in seven parts and focuses on three important phases in No Name's life: childhood (ages 8–11), adolescence (age 12), and manhood (age 16).

Part 1, receiving a name, childhood. A Choctaw boy is given the disparaging name of No Name by his father who regards him as unremarkable in every way.

Part 2, being loved, childhood. A girl called Whispering Wind sneaks up on No Name, kisses him wetly behind the ear, and confesses her love for him.

Part 3, becoming an adult, age 12. At age 12, No Name's baptism in the river by a Choctaw elder marks his passage from childhood to adulthood.

Part 4, an explosive encounter, age 12. On the night of his baptism, No Name finds his father alone in the house, sitting by a fire, smiling brightly. But his father's mood changes quickly. First praising his son for his newly-earned status as a Choctaw adult, he suddenly explodes, lashes out at his son with hateful words, and pushes him hard through the door. No Name lands heavily on the ground outside and starts sobbing.

Part 5, going to battle, age 16. The Choctaw Council declares war on the Creeks who set fire to some Choctaw houses one night without cause. At 16, having never fought in a war, young Choctaw men like No Name are eager to fight the Creeks and make names for themselves. The older Choctaw men hastily prepare the younger ones for battle, teaching them all they need to know about warfare; and on the night of their departure for Creek country, to complete their preparations as warriors, the young men dance spiritedly around a fire, chanting a war song.

The Creeks retreat to the mountains eastward and leave a trail that is easily followed. The trail ends suddenly at a cave surrounded by boulders. Convinced that the Creeks are inside and trapped, the Choctaw warriors make their move, rush forward and attack. But no Creeks are found in the cave, and soon the Choctaw warriors themselves are trapped, barred from leaving the cave by a heavy wooden gate heaved into place and set on fire by the Creeks who have come out of hiding.

Part 6, spiritual transmigration and homecoming, age 16. All but two Choctaw warriors die in the smoky cave. One is inside the cave, still alive; and one is No Name, lying by a boulder outside, downed by a hurled rock that prevented him from entering the cave with the other warriors. Now conscious again, No Name rushes to the burning gate and tries to pull it down, to free the warriors inside. But the gate is too heavy, falls back on him, and pins him to the ground.

The other warrior comes forward from the cave, approaches No Name, tries to free him from the gate but cannot; he touches No Name's temple with his fingertips, lifts his eyes upward, and accepts No Name's spirit into his body. No Name spends several days in the forest after that, wandering about, acclimating to his new body, and trying to understand what has happened to him. Once he is home, he goes straight to see Whispering Wind and helps her to recognize him as No Name.

Part 7, choosing a name, age 16. A week later, No Name and Whispering Wind are married, and when the time comes for the sole survivor of the recent war with the Creeks to choose a new name for himself, he chooses the good name of No Name.

Mythical Stories

The online *Oxford English Dictionary* defines a myth as a traditional story, typically involving supernatural beings or forces, which embodies and provides an explanation, etiology, or justification for something such as the early history of a society, a religious belief or ritual, or a natural phenomenon.[2] Mythical stories appear in seven novels and are summarized below in five thematic groups.

1.   Mythical Stories That Explain Distinctive Characteristics
2.   Mythical Stories About Earth Formations
3.   Mythical Stories About Firsts
4.   Mythical Stories About Little People
5.   A Mythical Story About a Sea Creature

Mythical Stories That Explain Distinctive Characteristics

Mythical stories that explain the distinctive snout of the lynx and head of the buzzard are shared in *DP* (29, 83). A story that explains the tamarack's lost power to retain its needles throughout the year is shared in *WP* (110). A story that explains the shadowy impression of a young girl on the full moon is shared in *HTS* (122).

Mythical Stories About Earth Formations

Mythical stories about the formation of North America and a specific arctic island appear in two novels. A mythical Shawnee story about the shaping of North America appears in *DP* (84). According to this mythical story, all of the world's original land was covered by water. The great continent of North America took shape when bits of earth were collected by birds and animals and deposited on the back of a great turtle.

A mythical Inuit story about the formation of Marble Island, a small white glassy island off the west coast of Hudson Bay near Rankin Inlet, is shared in *COTS* (108–9). According to this mythical story, a large ice floe was magically transformed by nature into an island to provide a new home for an old Inuit woman who found herself trapped on the ice floe and could not return home. The snowy white and glassy appearance of the new island resembled the original ice floe.

Mythical Stories About Firsts

Mythical stories about the first flute, the first wampum, and the first *Tekwaarathon* game appear in two novels. A mythical Lakota story about the first flute is shared in *LLM* (66). According to this mythical story, the Lakota people replicated a flute first crafted and put to use by a woodpecker. At some point in the past, this clever bird was observed hopping back and forth on a hollow branch with newly pecked holes. By stopping the holes with its feet, the woodpecker had learned to produce the most beautiful sounds while the wind whistled through the hollow center of the branch.

A mythical Mohawk story about the first wampum appears in *COTL* (88). According to this mythical story, a whole lakebed of small colorful shells, which became the first wampum, was collected and strung together by an important Mohawk man, a founding member of the League of Peace, who came upon a whole host of ducks and geese, feeding at the lake, that flew up suddenly and carried away the water.

A four-page mythical Mohawk story about the first *Tekwaarathon* (stick ball) game appears in *COTL* (99–102). This mythical story unfolds in three main parts. In the first part of the story, the four-legged animals and birds each challenge the other to a game of stick ball. In the second part of the story, each team meets with its members to agree on a game plan, and the bird team recruits two outcasts from the animal team, whom they furnish with wings, a bat, and a flying squirrel.

In the third part of the story, the two newly winged recruits play a pivotal role in the bird team's victory over the animal team in the stick ball match.

Mythical Stories About Little People

As noted in two sections of chapter 3, prominent individuals in six novels report memorable personal encounters with or briefly describe ancestral beings known as little people. The most descriptive account of these ancestral beings appears in *GOS* (103–10). Mythical stories about little people appear only in two novels.

In *LV*, while passing a tall rock cliff by canoe with her grandmother, Ray is reminded of a mythical encounter between a little (rock) man—called Memegwesi (little person) in Ojibwe—and an Ojibwe hunter (38–39). The Memegwesi was injured, and for nursing him back to health, the Ojibwe hunter received the magical gift of fish.

In *COTL*, during the annual strawberry thanksgiving event in her village, Otsi:stia recalls a mythical story about The Little Stone-Throwing People—called *Iakotinenioia'ks* in Mohawk—shared with her by the Clan Mother (23). In this mythical Mohawk story, a little Mohawk boy spends several days with a group of little people at their homes in caves along the river and for helping them in some undisclosed way receives a gift of a new fruit, called strawberries.

A Mythical Story About a Sea Creature

A mythical Inuit story about a strange sea creature with long hair and a deadly temperament appears in *COTS* (51–53). This strange creature called Nuliajuk sits on the ocean floor, as it has for as long as anyone can remember, and its long tangly hair moves back and forth with the currents and tides, trapping animals unexpectedly, and trying to shake them loose with tempestuous force.

Nuliajuk began life as a human being, the daughter of poor parents who expected her to marry and improve the family's fortunes. But when Nuliajuk repeatedly refused to marry, her parents set off in their boat to find a new place to live and left her behind to fend for herself. Nuliajuk followed them, swimming, caught up to them, grasped the side of the boat, and tried to climb aboard. But her father seized his ax, chopped off her fingers; and down she went to the bottom of the sea.

Stories About Animal Tricksters

According to *The Oxford Encyclopedia of Children's Literature* (Zipes 2006), a trickster tale is a distinctive type of traditional story that centers on a rule-breaking character. The rule-breaking speech and actions of such individuals are highly provocative and entertaining and help to clarify cultural traditions, values, and expectations.

Animal tricksters are identified in four novels: Rabbit (Choctaw), Raven (Sto: loh), and Azeban the raccoon (Abenaki). Rabbit is simply identified in the *NN* books (53; 149), and some basic information about the trickster/transformer Raven (Sto: loh) appears in *WG* (6–7).

A short trickster tale about Azeban the raccoon appears in *WP*, recalled by Saxso as he prepares for battle (140). In this well-known Abenaki trickster tale, Azeban approaches a great stone sitting on top of a steep hill. After a brief conversation with the stone, whom he calls his grandfather, Azeban ignores the stone's reservations about leaving the hilltop, smiles slyly to himself, and with a push sends the stone rolling downhill.

Evil Being Stories

Stories about evil beings appear in two novels. A Mohawk story that accounts for the transformation of an ordinary Mohawk man into a monster known as Skeleton Man appears in *SM* (3), and an Ojibwe story about a little girl's defeat of a *wiindigo* appears in *GOS* (159–65).

The Wiindigo Briefly

The *wiindigo*, described at length by Johnston (1996, i.e., *weendigo*), is known to many North American Indigenous peoples as the cannibal spirit, a supernatural human-like being that feasted on people. According to Johnston, the wiindigo was the most terrifying being known to Anishinaabe people, its appearance and behavior both ghastly and repulsive to them.

In terms of its basic bodily form, the weendigo resembled a human being but was distinctively skeletal in its appearance. It was five or more times taller than the average adult and gaunt to the point of emaciation. Its skin was ashy gray, its eyes sunken, and its teeth jaggedly sharp; and it stank like a decomposing body.

A *wiindigo*'s hunger for human flesh, human bones, and human blood was never satisfied. No sooner had a *wiindigo* captured a person, stripped him of his limbs, drank his blood, and devoured his body, head and all, then straightaway it hungered for a new victim, its stomach seemingly empty, its appetite unquenchably strong.

A *wiindigo* pursued its victims during the winter, and more so the end of winter when people's food supplies were low or had run out and people were thin and hungry. Wary wintertime travelers, observing sudden changes while traveling—trees mysteriously crackling, the air turning colder, or sudden blizzard-like conditions—would recognize the imminent attack of a *wiindigo* and quickly seek shelter.

The Little Girl and the Wiindigo

In an old-time Ojibwe village one winter, all signs pointed to an upcoming attack by a *wiindigo*. Whoever proved strong enough to light an old man's pipe without a match would be selected to defend the village against the *wiindigo*. All the villagers tried to light the pipe, but only a poor orphan girl proved strong enough to do so; and she wasted no time preparing for her fight. She knew exactly what to do.

As expected with the coming of a *wiindigo*, the weather grew suddenly cold, and in the nearby woods trees and rocks crackled and burst. Then the *wiindigo* appeared, a gigantic man covered with ice. Filled by the icy coldness that enveloped her, the orphan girl started to grow and soon was gigantic herself. She quickly dispatched the *wiindigo*'s dog, then killed the *wiindigo* with her copper rods.

A cup of hot tallow soup, prepared by the village women, restored the orphan girl to her normal size, and a helping of this same soup, poured down the throat of the dead *wiindigo*, restored life to the man whose being had been appropriated by the *wiindigo*, an ordinary Ojibwe man who from that point on provided gratefully for the orphan girl.

Eagle Stories

Eagle stories are identified collectively by Will in *WG* (7), but no details are shared about any specific story. The eagle stories identified by Will may include the Haida Eagle Story (see http://www.native-languages.org/ haidastory.htm), the eagle stories in *Indian Legends of the Pacific Northwest* (Clark 1975), or any of the stories with eagles in Adamson's (1934) collection of Coast Salish folktales. Bald Eagle is also a participant in the Bluejay Cycle epic stories in *Salish Myths and Legends: One People's Stories* (Thompson and Egesdal 2008).

Personal Stories

Prominent individuals in three novels share personal stories about themselves with family members. In *COTS,* The-man-with-no-eyebrows shares a personal hunting story about a huge bearded seal (42–43). In *BH,* Deydey shares an eerie story about his own personal encounter with ghosts (61–67), and Old Tallow shares her personal story of finding and rescuing Omakayas as a baby (232–37). In *TPY,* Nokomis shares a magical story about her personal encounter with two little people (103–10) and a childhood story about fishing in a forbidden place (134–38).

Family Stories

Will in *WG* and Nokomis in *TPY* recall or share stories about late family or kin group members. In *WG,* Will recalls the packing experiences of his late great-grandparents during the Cariboo Gold Rush in northern British Columbia (86–89). In *TPY,* Nokomis shares her personal knowledge with her granddaughter Omakayas about Old Tallow, her hard life as an orphan, and her development of great strength and ferocity (170–77).

WidelyCirculated Stories of Contemporary Renown

A widelycirculated story about Paaliaq and his fearless encounter with a polar bear appears in *COTS* (12–14). This remarkable encounter was witnessed by two Inuit hunters who promptly circulated the story upon their return to camp. Paaliaq was a young man at the time. He was hunting seals on the sea ice.

Inuit hunters often encountered polar bears on the sea ice. Paaliaq was ready for the encounter. The polar bear was large and fast. Paaliaq promptly released his dogs, who surrounded the bear, barking fiercely, baring their teeth, and nipping at the bear from behind. Paaliaq aimed his spear at the bear's chest, and tossed it; but the tip of the spear was too dull to penetrate the bear's thick skin, and the spear fell inertly in the snow.

The bear grew tired from the relentless pursuit of Paaliaq's dogs, each dog nipping at him from a different direction, turned, and sat down in the snow to protect its backside and legs from the dogs' damaging teeth. A moment passed before Paaliaq, looking for his spear, located it partly exposed beneath the seated bear.

All Paaliaq could do was to face his situation squarely with courage and resolve. He tossed his mitts aside, crept round his circle of dogs, approached the bear furtively from behind, dashed through his circle of dogs, grabbed the bear's tail, yanked it upward, and recovered his spear. Now face to face with the bear, who was ready to strike him with his huge paws, Paaliaq trust the spear in the bear's chest and killed it.

Indigenous Writing

Indigenous writing is identified in three novels. The use of Ojibwe or Cree syllabics is identified in *MT* (155). A Cree Bible, Cree Prayer Book, and Ojibwe Prayer Book are identified in *HTS* (15, 55). In *WG*, while recovering from surgery in the hospital, Will requests books from his family members— real books about residential schools, self-government, and nationhood by Indigenous writers (187).

NOTES

1. Oxford English Dictionary, s.v. "legend (n.)," accessed February 4, 2023, https://www.oed.com/legend.

2. Oxford English Dictionary, s.v. "myth (n.)," accessed February 4, 2023, https://www.oed.com/myth.

REFERENCES

Adamson, Thelma. *Folk-Tales of the Coast Salish*. New York: American Folklore Society, 1934.

Clark, Ella E., and Robert Bruce Inverarity. *Indian Legends of the Pacific Northwest.* Berkeley: University of California Press, 1953.

Day, Gordon, M. "The Western Abenaki Transformer." *Journal of the Folklore Institute,* vol. 13, no. 1 (1976): 75–89.

Gill, Sam D., and Irene F. Sullivan. 1992. *Dictionary of Native American Mythology.* Santa Barbara, CA: ABC-CLIO. February 4, 2023. https://search.ebscohost.com.

Johnston, Basil. *The Manitous: The Spiritual World of the Ojibway.* New York: Harper Perennial, 1996.

Powers, William K. *Oglala Religion.* Lincoln: University of Nebraska Press, 1975.

Rand, Silas Tertius. *Legends of the Micmacs.* Cambridge: University Press, 1893.

Stevens, James R. *Sacred Legends of the Sandy Lake Cree.* Toronto: McClelland and Stewart, 1971.

Thompson, Terry, and Steven Egesdal. *Salish Myths and Legends: One People's Stories.* Lincoln: University of Nebraska Press, 2008.

Zipes, Jack. *The Oxford Encyclopedia of Children's Literature.* Oxford: Oxford University Press, 2006.

Chapter 8

Group C

Family Life and Kinship

CHAPTER OVERVIEW

Indigenizing fictional world features in Group C and the Category of Family Life and Kinship are examined in this chapter. Four sets of Category 9 features are examined. In all, 13 indigenizing features are identified, described, and illustrated in this chapter.

9. Family Life and Kinship
   9.1 Family life: extended family households, sibling care, sibling avoidance, closeness to cousins
   9.2 Childbirth and childhood play: childbirth, childhood play
   9.3 Coming of age, courtships, and marriage: coming-of-age experiences, courtship, arranged marriages, respecting one's in-laws
   9.4 Kinship: clan membership, extending kinship to strangers, kinship with local animals

9. FAMILY LIFE AND KINSHIP

Specific Indigenous family life and kinship concerns are identified and described in varying detail by prominent individuals in 13 novels. These concerns relate to household membership, siblings, cousins, childbirth, childhood play, coming-of-age experiences, courtship, arranged marriages, in-laws, clan membership, and kinship connections to others. These family life and kinship concerns are distinguishing features of indigenized fictional worlds.

SET 9.1 FAMILY LIFE

Extended Family Households

An extended family household is a kinship group consisting of a nuclear family (parents and their children) and various relatives (e.g., grandparent, aunt, uncle, or cousin), all living in the same dwelling. Omakayas's household in *BH* is an extended family household consisting of her father (Deydey), mother (Yellow Knife), older sister (Angeline), younger brothers (Pinch and Neewo), and maternal grandmother (Nokomis).

In *BH* and *TPY*, Omakayas's extended family household also includes a close family friend called Old Tallow. In the *Birchbark House* series, Omakayas's household also includes other family friends such as Angeline's best friend Ten Snow and her husband Fishtail.

Sibling Care

Prominent older siblings in three novels provide care for younger siblings. In *LLM*, Lori acknowledges her Lakota duty as the oldest child in her family to provide care for her younger sibling Lana (7; see note below about Lakota relationships between cousins). In *COTS*, Wolverine cares for his baby sister (57, 80–81, 92); and in *BH,* Omakayas cares for both of her younger brothers (42–46, 212–15). Details about the care provided by Wolverine and Omakayas in the latter two novels follow.

An Example of Sibling Care Provided by an Inuit Boy

When his younger sister Little-Loved-One was a baby, Wolverine composed a special song for her while bouncing her on his knee. He honored her in his song, grateful to have a sister like her, and extolled her virtues of goodness, beauty, and competence. Growing up, Wolverine cared for his sister all the time, was her constant companion and babysitter, and transported her everywhere on his back.

When his sister was older and able to walk for increasingly longer periods of time on her own, Wolverine took his sister on regular outings up where falcons nested in the hills or to hidden places on the ground where freshly laid eggs could be found. Wolverine shared his knowledge with his sister about land and water birds—ptarmigans, buntings, geese, cranes, and more; and he chased hatchlings with his sister in the nesting grounds. He also liked to wrestle with his sister when she was big enough to wrestle.

An Example of Sibling Care Provided by an Ojibwe Girl

While still a child herself, age 7 or 8, Omakayas routinely takes care of her younger brothers Neewo and Pinch. In *BH* chapter 3, when her mother and other family members visit the trading post in the village, Omakayas takes charge of her brother Neewo until her mother returns later that morning. Her brother is fast asleep in his cradleboard, suspended from a tree near the house. Omakayas has only to be at hand for her brother, watch over him, rock him, and sing to him occasionally if needed. But her brother wakes suddenly from sleep, screams hysterically, and will not be subdued.

Omakayas responds quickly and her responsive actions pacify her brother. She removes him from his cradleboard and wet moss diaper, carries him to a sunny spot by the water, sits with him on a warm rock with a clear view of the lake, and gives him a stick to play with. Thereafter, she returns him promptly to his cradleboard, ties him in, and pops a small lump of maple sugar into his mouth to induce sleep.

In chapter 12, Omakayas treats her brother Pinch's burned feet with medicine from her grandmother's medicine pouch. Pinch rushes home from a playful hunting expedition, bumps carelessly into his father by the fireside, and spills his father's kettle of boiling sap on his feet. Omakayas takes swift action and treats her brother. She lays her brother on the ground, examines his feet, takes a packet of horsemint leaves from her grandmother's medicine pouch, makes a special paste from the leaves using a dab of animal grease, and applies the paste to his feet.

Sibling Avoidance

In *TPY* chapter 9, Omakayas notes a change in her younger brother Quill (formerly Pinch), who recently returned home after his captivity among the Bwaanag (92). Older now, Quill is taciturn and serious and follows the traditional Ojibwe practice of avoiding contact with his sisters.

Hallowell and Brown (1992) write that sibling avoidance (such as reflected in Omakayas's experience in *TPY*) was customary among the Ojibwe of Berens River, Manitoba. While same-sex siblings routinely interacted with each other and participated in common activities during and beyond adolescence, such was not the case for opposite-sex siblings. Opposite-sex siblings strictly avoided contact with each other.

Closeness to Cousins

In *LLM*, in the traditional Lakota way, Lori's relationship with her first cousin Lana is properly understood as a relationship between sisters not cousins, as the two teenage girls are the offspring of sisters (7).

In two of the three *Birchbark House* novels, Omakayas spends a lot of time with her cousins. In *BH*, Omakayas's springtime sugar camp is very close to her cousins' camp, and the group of four female cousins spend most of their free time together, roaming between camps and playing games with each other (208). In *GOS*, two years later, the four cousins live in close proximity from summer to spring, and they spend even more time together, playing and engaging in seasonal activities with their parents.

SET 9.2 CHILDBIRTH AND CHILDHOOD PLAY

Childbirth

A detailed account of Wolverine's delivery is provided in *COTS* (8–9). Wolverine's mother Can't-see delivered baby Wolverine alone in her igloo when her husband was out on the ice hunting seals in the spring. Can't-see prepared her igloo for Wolverine's birth. She positioned herself comfortably and warmly on a caribou skin, propped herself up on several rolled skins, pushed her new baby into the world, tidied up, then disposed of her caribou-skin bedding.

Childhood Play

Prominent children in six novels, including all three novels in the *Birchbark House* series, engage in childhood play. While playing, children in three of the six novels enact the adult role of mother (*COTS* 59; *GOS* 11, 38), hunter (*COTS* 59, 77; *TPY* 1–2), warrior (*GOS* 114–15), and war chief (*GOS* 115). Children in four of the six novels engage in childhood play by sliding down a snowy slope with or without a toboggan (*GOS* 166, *HTS* 103), skating (*HTS* 155, *SW* 208), climbing a tree (*GOS* 40–41), and creating rock children (*BH* 38).

SET 9.3 COMING OF AGE, COURTSHIP, AND MARRIAGE

Coming-of-Age Experiences

In *COTL* and *GOS*, adolescent members of the Mohawk and Ojibwe nations contemplate or are presently involved in specific experiences that mark their transition from childhood to adulthood. Coming-of-age experiences for Mohawk boys are described in *COTL* (32–33). Coming-of-age experiences for Ojibwe children and for one adolescent girl are described in *GOS* (59–60, 63–66, 226–32).

A Mohawk Coming-of-Age Event

In *COTL* chapter 3, eleven-year-old Ohkwa'ri contemplates the coming- of-age tradition that is relevant for all adolescent boys in his village. Mohawk tradition dictates that when boys reach puberty at roughly age 13, they must move out of their family's longhouse, separate themselves from their mothers, and undergo a year of hard training that will prepare them for manhood.

Ojibwe Children's Quests for Spirit Protectors

In *GOS* chapter 4, as Omakayas, her sister, and grandmother all work diligently on a deer hide, removing the hair, preparing the hide for trade, Omakayas's thoughts turn from the task at hand and deer hide to spiritual matters and the quest all Ojibwe children undertake at her age to acquire a lifelong spirit protector (59–60).

In such quests for a spirit protector, most Ojibwe children spent four days and nights in the woods, often alone and without eating, seeking a personal communication with the spirit world, a spiritual vision, with their faces blackened by charcoal to signify their intentions. To expedite such visions, some children chose to fast for the duration of their quests. Questing children elicited pity from the spirit world and over the course of four days were spoken to by individual spirits.

Omakayas acquired her spirit protector, Bear, differently than most children her age. Bear first appeared to her in a dream when she was very little (*TPY* 37), then last winter, while grieving the loss of her baby brother who died suddenly of smallpox, Bear spoke to her in a dream. Bear had heard her grieving that time, pitied her, and offered himself as her spirit protector.

In a private conversation with her brother Pinch later in chapter 4, Omakayas acknowledges that spending time in the woods alone without food and communicating with spirits frightens most children. But she reassures

Pinch that his forthcoming vision and acquisition of a spirit protector will strengthen him.

Courtship

In the field of cultural anthropology, courtship is generally understood as an interval of time in a couple's relationship, prior to marriage, when each shows romantic interest in the other, spends time with each other, bonds with each other, seeking the likely outcome of marriage. In three novels, young men seek possible marriage with specific young women using homemade flutes and traditional courting music.

In *TPY*, Omakayas learns from her mother that long ago her father won her mother's heart by playing traditional Ojibwe courting music for her on his flute (141). In *WG*, Will imagines his mother and grandmother standing by the window many years ago, leaning against each other, listening to the plaintive music coming from his father's courting flute outside (167). His mother and grandmother take stock of Will's father, appraising his suitability as a husband, sharing their thoughts with each other softly, and appearing to merge, as the music trails off.

In *LLM*, Lori learns from her grandfather, an experienced flute maker and flutist, that traditional Lakota flutes played a key role in courtship (66). When he was a young man himself, as was true for many generations of young men before him, he expressed his interest in a young woman by courting her with his flute, standing outside her tipi and playing his flute for her. A woman who sought to encourage her suitor, and had the approval of her parents to do so, spent time with the man outside, wrapped with him in a blanket.

Arranged Marriages

In arranged marriages, individuals are commonly selected as spouses for each other by their parents. Such was the case for Wolverine's parents and Wolverine himself in *COTL*. In chapter 5, Wolverine's father visits the shaman Paaliaq shortly after the birth of his daughter and acknowledges the custom of arranged marriages among Inuit people like him: all marriages were arranged at birth by a baby's parents (24). His own marriage to Can't-see was arranged that way; and when they were grown, he collected his wife from her parents' home, took her away, and started a family with her.

Although Wolverine's parents seek to arrange a marriage between their baby son and the shaman's baby daughter Breath, an arrangement cannot be secured until the two children reach adolescence and show themselves to be amicable and well matched for marriage (88–90). While observing their adolescent children catching and cleaning fish one summer, all four parents wholeheartedly and gratefully agree that the two young people are a good match and should be married.

In *DBDP*, Danny Blackgoat is greatly surprised when his devoted friend Rick, the white delivery driver who delivered him to Fort Davis in the first *Danny Blackgoat* novel *DBNP*, invites Danny to marry his daughter Jane. Rick's wife is Navajo, and Danny is very honored by the arranged marriage proposal from Rick and gratefully accepts (52).

Respecting One's In-laws

In *COTS* chapter 20, Wolverine is held captive on Marble Island a great distance from home by adverse spiritual forces unleashed on him by his soon-to-be father-in-law Paaliaq. But despite his present situation, as desolate as it appears, he rightly calms himself and resists responding in kind, returning a curse with a curse (124). Wolverine reminds himself that Inuit custom prevents him from thinking or speaking badly about his in-laws and obliges him to hold his in-laws in high regard, to honor and respect them above all others, even his parents.

SET 9.4 KINSHIP

Clan Membership

Clans are important kinship groups in three novels. In the first chapter of *COTL*, Ohkwa'ri notes his membership in the Bear Clan, one of three Mohawk clans identified in a prefatory figure. Anthropologists define a clan formally as a unilineal kinship group whose members trace their descent to a common ancestor (Nanda and Warms 2004). Members of all three Mohawk clans including the Bear, Wolf, and Turtle Clans trace their descent through a female member. In *WG* chapter 5, Will's aunt speaks candidly to him about Sto: loh clans, comparing clan-based and democratic principles (45–47).

In *BH* chapter 5, while lying in the underbrush eavesdropping on Albert and Fishtail's disturbing report to her father about the increasing number of white people invading Ojibwe lands, Omakayas's thoughts turn momentarily to clans (79). Omakayas identifies her father's clan as the Catfish Clan. According to the Leech Lake Band of Ojibwe website, members of the Ojibwe Nation today belong to one of the 21 clans shown below.

Uj-e-jauk, Crane
Man-un-aig, Catfish
Mong, Loon

Ma-kwa, Bear
Waub-ish-ash-e, Marten
Addick, Reindeer
Mah-een-gun, Wolf
Ne-baun-aub-ay, Merman
Ke-noushay, Pike
Be-sheu, Lynx
Me-gizzee, Eagle
Che-she-gwa, Rattlesnake
Mous, Moose
Muk-ud-a-shib, Black Duck or Cormorant
Ne-kah, Goose
Numba-bin, Sucker
Numa, Sturgeon
Ude-kumaig, White Fish
Amik, Beaver
Gy-aushk, Gull
Ka-kaik, Hawk

Extending Kinship to Strangers

Kinship is extended to strangers in two novels. In *LLM*, Lori recalls reading a story about a white boy who was adopted by Lakota people a long time ago (49). In *BH*, Omakayas learns about her own adoption from Old Tallow (232–37). In *GOS*, Omakayas gains an adopted brother and cousin when a group of ragged Ojibwe strangers arrives at her family's summer camp (7).

Kinship With Local Animals

Kinship relationships with buzzards, panthers, and bears are identified in three novels. In *DBRRTF*, while addressing a group of soldiers who have come from Fort Sumner to replenish their water supply in the hills, Danny Blackgoat's grandfather likens himself to a buzzard, aiming to divert attention from his grandson's whereabouts beneath the soldier's wagon (78).

In *SRC*, Funi Man teaches Lil Mo about panthers, their ancestral connection and special importance to Choctaw peoples (80). Panthers, explains Funi Man, are the most highly regarded animals for Choctaw peoples. Panthers are inhabited by ancestral spirits that protect good Choctaw people. Panthers bring warnings and blessings to those they encounter: warnings of forthcoming dangers and blessings of truthfulness.

In *WP* chapter 23, Saxso's quiet bear-like movement through the forest reminds him of his kinship ties to bears (127–28). A family legend tells of an ancestor, a boy, who was stolen from his parents by a mother bear whose cubs were recently killed by a careless hunter. The bear took care of the boy for some time, lived with him in a cave, provided for him, and taught him all the things he needed to know to fend for himself when grown. Eventually the boy was rescued and returned to his family, but it took him some time to stop thinking of himself as a bear and resume his life as a human.

REFERENCES

Adamson, Thelma. *Folk-Tales of the Coast Salish*. New York: American Folklore Society, 1934.

Hallowell, A. Irving, and Jennifer S. H. Brown. 1992. *The Ojibwa of Berens River, Manitoba: Ethnography into History*. Fort Worth: Harcourt Brace Jovanovich College Publishers, 1992.

Leech Lake Band of Ojibwe. "Minnesota Chippewa Tribe Student Handbook, Chapter 1." *Legal Department.* February 4, 2023. www.llojibwe.org.

Nanda, Serena, and Richard L. Warms. *Cultural Anthropology.* 8th ed. Belmont, CA: Wadsworth/Thomson Learning, 2004.

Chapter 9

Group D

Destruction and Restoration

CHAPTER OVERVIEW

Indigenizing fictional world features in Group D and the Categories of Destruction, Protection, Restoration, and Recovery are examined in this final chapter. Category 10, 11, and 12 features are examined in four, two, and one set(s) respectively. In all, 25 indigenizing features are identified, described, and illustrated. The chapter includes some final words that bring the book to a close.

10. Divestments, Denigration, Subjugation, Disease
    10.1 Forced appropriation, moves, separations, sterilization, material appropriation: material appropriation, forced relocation from homeland, forced removal from homeland, forced separation of children from parents, forced sterilization, material deprivation
    10.2 Cultural denigration, disdain, identity concealment
    10.3 Harassment, subjugation, brutality
    10.4 Disease: smallpox, diabetes
11. Sovereignty, Defense, and Leadership
    11.1 Sovereignty and defense: sovereignty, defense of sovereignty, defense of homes and homelands
    11.2 Leadership: clan mothers, chiefs, councils, elders, societies
12. Restoration and Recovery: recovery, restoration, cultural pride

10. DIVESTMENTS, DENIGRATION, SUBJUGATION, DISEASE

Prominent individuals or whole communities of Indigenous people in 16 novels experience the loss of ancestral lands, natural resources, or personal possessions; various types of mistreatment; the forced concealment of one's Indigenous identity; and the fatal or debilitating effects of smallpox or diabetes. These common experiences of divestment, denigration, subjugation, and disease are distinguishing features of indigenized fictional worlds.

SET 10.1 FORCED APPROPRIATION, MOVES, SEPARATIONS, STERILIZATION, AND DEPRIVATION

Material Appropriation

According to the online *American Heritage Dictionary*, to appropriate means to take possession of or make use of exclusively for oneself, often without permission.[1] Key resources owned by Indigenous peoples—land, water, and grain—are appropriated by the United States or Canadian government in four novels.

In *TPY* chapter 7, while hiding in the underbrush, trying to avoid detection by a passing group of warriors from the plains, long-standing enemies of Ojibwe people, Omakayas recalls her father's recent comment about their newest and deadliest enemies—the white settlers, who continue to appropriate ancestral lands from Indigenous people like the Ojibwe (76).

In *WP* chapter 7, Saxso's village, an Abenaki settlement, is attacked at night by a large company of soldiers called the Bostonian Rangers (i.e., Roger's Rangers), who seek to destroy the village and its inhabitants. Saxso survives the attack by hiding in a nearby ravine. In chapter 8, he returns to the village and describes the devastation and plunder. The village lies in ruins. Many farm animals are dead. The village storehouses have been plundered. Many precious bags of corn were carried off by the soldiers (53).

In *MT* chapter 3 "Story: Part One," Miig recounts a period in Anishnaabe [*sic*] and Canadian history when Americans (America), faced with a shortage of fresh water, appropriated water resources from the lakes and rivers on Anishnaabe ancestral lands (24). In *HR* chapter 7 "Wood," Grandpa Louis recalls the many log cabins and small bark houses belonging to local Indigenous people that were appropriated and demolished by company workers building the Sacandaga Reservoir (54).

Forced Relocation from Homeland

An account of the forced relocation of a specific family or community of Abenaki or Anishnaabe (Anishinaabe) people from their ancestral homeland now or in recent memory appears in four novels. In *GOS* chapter 16, Fishtail reports that the United States government is forcing Omakayas's family and their Ojibwe neighbors to leave their homes on the Island of the Golden-Breasted Woodpecker, cede their lands to European settlers, and relocate westward to live among the people of the plains (234–35). At the end of chapter 16, Omakayas and her family embark by canoe for Lake of the Woods. The family's travels northward by boat, which span a great distance, are recounted in *TPY*.

In *WP* chapter 2, Saxso recalls details about a series of events that forced his ancestors to abandon their homeland and beautiful village by the falls (now Turner's Falls). Details about these events, including a massacre of his ancestors at Turner's Falls, were related to Saxso personally by his great-grandfather Beaver's Tail, who witnessed the massacre firsthand as a boy (10–15).

In *MT* chapter 3, Miig reports that many Anishnaabe communities were forced to relocate from their homelands when life-sustaining water resources were appropriated by Americans and depleted (24–25).

Forced Removal from Homeland

The forced removal of whole communities of Navajo people from the Canyon de Chelly in New Mexico in 1863–1864 during the Carson invasion is described in detail in the first two chapters of *DBNP* (1–15). In chapter 1, from a small cave on the canyon wall that offers a wide view of the canyon, Danny spots a hundred soldiers in the distance riding towards his family's hogan. The soldiers seize his father, mother, and sister, quickly seize Danny when he appears, bind all of them around the waist, kill the family sheep, burn down the house, and hold the family as prisoners in their own corral.

By the following evening, four hundred Navajo men, women, and children have likewise been rounded up by the soldiers and imprisoned in the same corral as Danny and his family. All were removed forcibly from their homes, delivered roughly to the Blackgoat corral, and witnessed the destruction of their homes and animals. On the third day of their captivity, all are given a small helping of dry bread and water, then marched roughly by foot to Fort Sumner 300 miles away.

Forced Separation of Children from Parents

The forced separation of Indigenous children from their parents is reported by old Indigenous men in two novels. In *MT* chapter 3 "Story: Part One," Miig reports the many losses experienced by Anishinaabe children when they were removed from their homes by the newcomers (i.e., Canadian government) and forced to attend their schools (23–24). In *HR* chapter 15 "Law," Sonny's grandfather reports that Indigenous children in Vermont, their home state, were often taken away from their parents and offered for adoption after a sterilization bill was passed in 1931 (122, 126, 132–33).

Forced Sterilization

Young Indigenous women like Sonny's late grandmother Sophie in *HR*, as reported in chapter 15 and the author's note, were involuntarily sterilized by doctors in free medical clinics established in Vermont when the sterilization bill became law in 1931 (122–24). Sonny learns from his grandfather in chapter 15 that his grandmother lost the ability to bear children after visiting a free clinic. Only one of her three children survived infancy, so she visited a nearby clinic expecting the doctors to help her to bear healthy children. The doctors sterilized her instead.

Material Deprivation

According to the online *Merriam-Webster Dictionary*, to deprive means to withhold something from.[2] In *DBNP*, on his long walk to Fort Sumner as a prisoner, Danny Blackgoat is deprived of drinking water (17) and medical attention (30).

SET 10.2 CULTURAL DENIGRATION, DISDAIN, AND IDENTITY CONCEALMENT

Cultural Denigration

According to the online *American Heritage Dictionary*, to denigrate means to attack the character or reputation of, speak ill of, or defame;[3] and to defame means to damage the reputation, character, or good name of (someone) by slander or libel.[4] Culturally denigrating references are commonly referred to as ethnic insults.

As noted in *An Encyclopedia of Swearing*, "Ethnic insults are the most obvious linguistic manifestation of xenophobia and prejudice against

Table 9.1. Ethnic insults identified in eight novels

Reference	Target	Defamer	Novel	Page
damned Indians	Carrie	shopper	WIB	75
dumb Indians	Navajo prisoners	soldier, prisoner, guard	DBNP	9, 48, 128
savages	Navajo people	soldiers	DBNP	48
bloodthirsty savages	Abenaki people	English newcomers	WP	16
cannibals	Abenaki people	enemies	WP	124
thieves	home owners	construction workers	HR	56
Geronimo, Tonto	Armie	classmates	DP	3
gypsies	Louis	town boys	MTTT	2
dirty Indian gypsies	Louis	town boys	MTTT	2
blamed tramps	Louis	town boys	MTTT	2
Chief	Louis, Will, Armie	new recruit, teammates, classmate	MTTT, WG, DP	20, 88
Injun	Louis, Danny	new recruit, soldier	MTTT, DBNP	20, 30
smoked meat	Will	teammates	WG	83
buffalo dung	Bobby	neighborhood boy	NN	89

out-groups. They are usually based on malicious, ironic, or humorous distortions of the target group's identity or 'otherness'" (Hughes 2015, 146).

Prominent Indigenous individuals are personally or collectively denigrated because of their cultural otherness in eight novels. Table 9.1 identifies the prominent individuals singled out and defamed.

Disdain

According to the online *Oxford English Dictionary*, to disdain means to regard or treat with contempt.[5] Disdained individuals are regarded as inferior, worthless, or despicable and often treated abusively.

In *DBNP* chapter 6, Danny Blackgoat is disdained—regarded and treated with contempt—by the guards and a prisoner on the first full day of his imprisonment at Fort Sumner (47–48). In a cotton field near the fort, where prisoners like Danny are forced to pick cotton all day, five guards single out Danny, aim their guns at him and threaten to blow him apart if he makes a wrong move. Then an older prisoner calls Danny a dumb Indian, spits on him, and knocks him to the ground.

Ancestral Identity Concealment

In the closing chapters of the novel *HR*, chapters 14 and 15 "Roots" and "Laws," Sonny learns from his grandfather about the need for Indigenous peoples past and present to protect themselves and their loved ones by concealing their Indigenous identities, their ancestral roots (115–29). In an intimate conversation with his grandfather in chapter 14, Sonny learns that his grandfather and parents are Indigenous people, part Abenaki and part Mohican, and have always concealed their Indigenous identities to avoid mistreatment by others and to have more opportunities in life.

SET 10.3 HARASSMENT, SUBJUGATION, AND BRUTALITY

Harassment

According to the online *American Heritage Dictionary*, to harass means to subject a person to hostile or prejudicial remarks or actions.[6] In *WIB*, Carrie's birth father Harold informs her that he and other members of their reserve are commonly harassed by the police because they are Mohawk. In chapter 10, Carrie witnesses this harassment firsthand, traveling to an off-reserve store in her father's car, when her father is dubiously pulled over by a police officer, treated rudely, and fined for speeding (74).

Subjugation

According to the online *American Heritage Dictionary*, to subjugate means to bring under control, especially by military force; to make subordinate to the dominion of something else.[7] In seven novels, an individual or group of Inuit, Mohawk, Choctaw, Abenaki, or Navajo people are subjugated by a curse, negligence, witchcraft, or capture.

In *COTS* chapter 5, the Inuit shaman Paaliaq curses his friend's son Wolverine in a fit of anger and from that point on subjugates the boy to the powers of the spirit world (25). Years later in chapter 17, while hunting whales with his father far out to sea, Wolverine, now a young man, is prevented from returning home to the mainland by a perpetually stormy sea produced by the shaman's curse and his *tuurnngaq* (106–13).

In *COTL* chapter 7, when Otsi:stia learns that the upcoming Tekwaarathon match between her village and another will help to restore an elder's health, her thoughts turn briefly to some traditional ways that people are healed in her village and then to two common ways that people are subjected to sickness or death. Hunters who neglect to honor an animal for its sacrifice often fall sick, subjected to the corrective powers of animal spirits (91). Other villagers occasionally fall sick or even die at the bidding of witches (92).

Unidentified witches subject Mohawk people to sickness or death in *COTL*. In *SRC*, an identified witch, banned from entering Choctaw town, takes control of Lil Mo in the woods and causes him to lose all sense of himself (175–79). The witch is an old man who derives his witchly powers from owls. Lil Mo is compelled to sing and dance wildly, mesmerized by a special fan made of owl feathers, and is then commanded to subjugate others by winding strands of people's hair around the fan's handle.

In *WP* chapter 9, Saxso learns from a friend that three family members, his mother and two sisters, are among the Abenaki people whom the Bostonian Rangers captured and led away during their nighttime attack on Saxso's village (59). In all three *Danny Blackgoat* series novels hundreds of Navajo people are captured by soldiers, marched by foot to Fort Sumner, and imprisoned there for the entire series of novels. Danny Blackgoat himself is imprisoned at both Forts Davis and Sumner.

Brutality

Indigenous people in four novels whose homelands are situated in southwestern and eastern states are treated brutally by American soldiers, fellow prisoners, bounty hunters, and government authorities. In *DBNP*, Danny Blackgoat is treated brutally many times in the novel. Two examples are particularly noteworthy. In chapter 4, he is tied prostrate and bloody to the back of a horse by the soldiers who captured him, paraded back and forth along a long line of Navajo prisoners removed from their homeland, and told by the soldiers that they will treat his body brutally when he is dead (26–30).

Midway through the novel, while imprisoned at Fort Davis, Danny is treated brutally again, this time by a fellow prisoner, Mr. Dime, the same prisoner who treated him with contempt in chapter 6. In chapter 11, now seeking to kill Danny, Mr. Dime places a live rattlesnake in a loosely closed bag in Danny's bed, hidden under the covers (80). The snake strikes Danny that night and nearly kills him.

In *WP*, as noted in Set 10.1 above, Saxso both recalls and witnesses the brutal treatment of Abenaki people by American soldiers. He recalls the slaughter of a whole Abenaki village of women and children and witnesses the complete destruction of his own village. In *WITD*, Maddy connects the gruesome decapitation of dogs and cats in her neighborhood with the brutal scalping of Indigenous peoples by American bounty hunters in previous centuries (110–11). In *HR*, Sonny learns from his grandfather about the brutal sterilization of his grandmother Sophie (see Set 10.1 above).

SET 10.4 DISEASE

Smallpox

The devastating effects of smallpox in the lives of Omakayas, her family members, members of her household, family friends, and neighbors are described in all three novels in the *Birchbark House* series. Personal stories of childhood hardships from the past specific to Omakayas and Old Tallow caused by smallpox are recounted by Old Tallow in *BH* (1–2, 232–37) and Nokomis in *TPY* (171).

In *BH* chapter 10, Omakayas's parents, grandmother, sister, and brothers all fall ill with smallpox, and their individual experiences are described by Omakayas who is not infected with the disease (143–54). A visiting voyageur and his hosts, including Angeline's best friend Ten Snow, all die from smallpox in rapid succession (143, 150).

Omakayas cares for her baby brother Neewo when her mother falls ill, but soon her brother falls ill too. For several days she cares for her brother in the main house where all her family members are gathered. Only two of them are well: Omakayas and her grandmother. Omakayas holds her brother, a baby, lovingly in her arms, holds him like that for several nights, bathes him with cool water, but she is not able to save him. He dies in her arms (148–49). In *GOS*, Omakayas refers to this terrible winter in 1847 as the smallpox winter, that terrible winter when she lost her precious baby brother Neewo (fore matter x).

Diabetes

In *WIB* chapter 14, when her grandmother collapses in the kitchen after nicking her finger with a knife, Carrie quickly deduces from recent events that her grandmother suffers from diabetes and needs insulin. The main road leading to and from the reserve is blocked. Tensions between the Ontario police and people of Kanehsatake are mounting. Carrie grabs the phone and makes two urgent calls, one to her aunt, and the other to her adoptive mother, a doctor (98–99).

Collecting her mother from off the reserve with the main road blocked is challenging. But with her grandmother's car and her sister as a guide, Carrie delivers her mother to her grandmother's house with impressive speed. Shortly after their arrival, her mother confirms that the old woman is diabetic and collapsed from diabetic shock. Carrie's mother's quick diagnosis and prompt administration of insulin saves Carrie's grandmother's life (100–102).

11. SOVEREIGNTY, DEFENSE, AND LEADERSHIP

Prominent individuals or whole communities of Indigenous people in 13 novels exercise or defend their sovereign rights as (members of) an identified Indigenous Nation, defend their family homes or ancestral homelands, or submit to the authority of an Indigenous leader such as a clan mother, chief, or elder. Fictional worlds are indigenized by explicit and substantive references to Indigenous sovereignty, defensive actions against invaders, and Indigenous leadership.

SET 11.1 SOVEREIGNTY AND DEFENSE

Sovereignty

In *SRC* chapter 15, Martha Tom's mother Ella informs Lil Mo's father Lavester about Choctaw nationhood and laws and assures him that he and his family members are safe on the Choctaw side of the river. Lavester, his wife, and two children are enjoying their second night of freedom in Choctaw town when Ella enters their temporary shelter bearing food.

Ella informs Lavester that the plantation owners, who claim to own him and his family members, cannot impose that claim on the Choctaw side of the river; and that the people of Choctaw town are recognized as a nation by the United States government, live by their own set of laws, and protect themselves and their guests (74–75).

Defense of Sovereignty

Moreover, in *SRC* chapter 15, Ella assures Lavester in the same conversation that the plantation owners have no legal rights on this side of the river, that the Choctaw Nation owns the land, and protects their land and nationhood with arms (74–75).

Defense of Homes and Homelands

Members of Indigenous communities in two novels take action to defend their homes or homelands against a military attack or foreign government appropriation of Indigenous resources. In *WP* chapter 4, members of Saxso's village refuse to be driven from their homes by soldiers, agree to barricade themselves in the Council Hall, will wait for the soldiers to launch their attack, then defend their village with muskets (31).

In *NN* chapter 14, while walking home from the park, Bobby learns from his best friend Johnny about a lawsuit brought by Bobby's own Choctaw Nation against the state of Oklahoma over water rights on Choctaw lands. Johnny (Cherokee) mentions the lawsuit while talking about his uncle, a lawyer, who works for the Choctaw Nation in Durant and filed a lawsuit against the state of Oklahoma when it attempted to appropriate water from lakes on Choctaw lands (94–95).

SET 11.2 LEADERSHIP

Clan Mothers

In *COTL* chapter 1, Ohkwa'ri identifies his grandmother She Opens the Sky as the oldest of three Clan Mothers in the big longhouse (11). According to Ohkwa'ri, Clan Mothers select chiefs as village leaders, endorse or forbid proposed raids on neighboring villages or declarations of war, and aim to ensure that all clan members follow the Great Law (15). In chapter 2, in her observations about her own longhouse, which houses the Bear Clan, Otsi:stia notes that her grandmother, in her role as Clan Mother, serves as the head of the Bear Clan and has charge of the longhouse (21–22).

Ohkwa'ri and Otsi:stia's understandings about their grandmother's key leadership role as Clan Mother in their village (i.e., Kanatsiohareke Village, c. 1490) are supported by Jacobs (1991). Jacobs writes that Clan Mothers were the most respected members of their villages and held the highest positions of authority. They selected chiefs, monitored the chiefs' activities, reminded the chiefs to follow the Great Law, and removed chiefs if warranted. Clan Mothers advised and directed warriors, made life-and-death decisions about captives, and settled General Council disputes.

Moreover, Otsi:stia notes in chapter 10 that her grandmother played a key role in village corn planting decisions. As Clan Mother, her grandmother

Table 9.2. Indigenous leaders identified in seven novels

Chief	Nation	Novel	Page(s)
Chief Pyle	Choctaw	*NN*	95
General Ely S. Parker	Seneca	*MTTT*	171
the chief	Sto: loh	*WG*	124
Pine Tree chiefs	Mohawk	*COTL*	8
Chief Joseph-Louis Gill	Abenaki	*WP*	13, 20
Miskabines	Ojibwe	*GOS*	3
rice chiefs	Ojibwe	*BH*	95

identified stretches of forest that needed to be cleared for new corn fields and even tasted the soil in certain locations to ascertain its quality (115).

Chiefs

Indigenous leaders designated as chiefs by members of their Indigenous communities are identified collectively or individually in seven novels. As shown in table 9.2, chiefs are identified for specific Choctaw, Seneca, Sto: loh, Mohawk, Abenaki, and Ojibwe communities.

Councils

Specific Indigenous councils are identified in three novels. Choctaw Councils are identified in *NN* (62) and *SRC* (165), and the Narragansett Tribal Council is identified in *WITD* (30).

Elders

Elders are identified in seven novels. In *WP*, an Abenaki elder, Nanagonsikon, is individually named (28). In *TPY*, *WG*, *COTL*, and *NMNN*, Ojibwe, Sto: loh, Mohawk, and Choctaw elders are identified (47; 31; 64; 108). In *MT*, members of Francis's Indigenous group are referred to collectively as elders (20), and in *WITD*, a national assembly of elders across North America is identified (105).

Societies

A Lakota society of women called Wiyan Omimiceye is identified in *LLM* (15). This society is based in a church and consists mostly of Lakota grand-mothers. Society members make and sell quilts that help fund various con-gregational projects.

12. RECOVERY AND RESTORATION

Prominent individuals in seven novels recover a person or thing of great value to them, have a restorative experience, or speak proudly about an Indigenous heritage. The recovery of ancestral bones, captured loved ones, or a signifi-cant cultural experience that ceased to be viable at some point in the past; the return of a family member, a restored cultural practice previously outlawed, a restored engagement, restored states of calmness and peace; and expressions of pride about one's Indigenous identity are distinguishing features of indigenized fictional worlds.

Recovery

According to the online *American Heritage Dictionary*, to recover means to get back.[8] In *LLM* chapter 8, Lori recovers the cultural experience of a buffalo hunt at the annual Buffalo Roundup (79, 91). In *WITD* chapter 5, Maddy's dad recovers their ancestors' bones from museums and colleges for reburial (30). In *WP* chapters 17–27, Saxso rescues (recovers) his mother and sisters from a guarded military camp many miles from their village (96–149). In *TPY* chapter 8, Old Tallow recounts Deydey's efforts to recover his son Quill from captivity among the Bwaanag (82–85).

Restoration

According to the online *American Heritage Dictionary*, to restore means (i) to bring back to an original or normal condition; (ii) to bring back into existence or use.[9] A family, kin group, betrothal, favorable traveling conditions, and a key cultural practice are restored (i.e., returned) in four novels. In *WIB* chapter 13, Carrie, a member of the Mohawk Nation, returns to live with her biological family in Kahnawake after a long separation (93). In *TPY* chapter 13, Miskobines and his son Animikiins are freed by the Bwaanag and return to live with (i.e., are restored to) their kin group (137–39).

In *COTS* chapter 14, the shaman Paaliaq restores the betrothal between Breath and Wolverine (93), then removes the curse and that restores order to the sea and allows Wolverine to travel home (118). In *LLM* chapter 9, a powwow is held (i.e., restored to its rightful place) at the annual Buffalo Roundup (92). In *NN* chapter 8, the Choctaw chief in Mr. Robison's story identifies forgiveness as the means by which peace relations are restored (53).

Calmness and peace are restored in three novels. In *COTS* chapter 10, the shaman Paaliaq restores peace to Nuliajuk, as only shamans can do (53). In *NN* chapter 13, peace is restored between neighborhood boys (90). In *WIB* chapter 15, peace is (restoratively) offered to the army officers by Mohawk warriors in Kahnawake (108).

Cultural Pride

A prominent individual in two novels is instructed to be or extolled for being proud of her Indigenous heritage and identity. In *WIB* chapter 10, Carrie's grandmother instructs Carrie to be proud of who she is—a Mohawk (Indian)—when a customer at the grocery store denigrates her and her grandmother, calling them damned Indians (75). In *LLM* chapter 12, at her wake service, Lana is extolled by a classmate for being proud of her American Indian heritage and proudly making it known to everyone at their school (114).

CONCLUSION

This book has identified, described, and illustrated 12 categories of features—158 individual features in all—that distinguish the fictional worlds presented to readers ages 10–16 in 24 novels by Indigenous authors. As noted at the start of this book, these 12 categories and the larger organizational structure of four large groups of features, Groups A–D (shown below), are the result of an intense and highly focused analysis of the selected novels using Systemic-Functional Linguistics and conceptual and personal understandings about Indigenous peoples and their experiences published by Indigenous scholars and writers.

Group A (1–3). Time, Tribal History, Ancestry (12 features)

Group B (4–7). Cultural Beliefs, Values, Events, Traditions (81 features)

Group C (8–9). Language Use, Stories, Storytelling, Family Life, Kinship (28 features)

Group D (10–12). Destruction and Restoration (37 features)

The inventory of indigenizing fictional world features offered in this book is intended to be used as a heuristic or instructional framework by teachers and students in middle and high school grades for exploring Indigenous novels and the fictional world experiences of Indigenous young people past and present. Such explorations will surely help Indigenous students to better understand themselves as Indigenous people and help non-Indigenous students to gain transformative understandings about the personal and collective experiences of Indigenous peoples in the United States and Canada.

This book has focused on the development of a framework for collaborative classroom explorations of Indigenous novels and indigenized fictional worlds in middle and high school humanities courses. The next book will focus more narrowly on a subset of novels from this first book and specific resources that teachers can use to guide their students' exploration of these indigenized fictional worlds collaboratively.

NOTES

1. American Heritage Dictionary, s.v. "appropriate (v.)," accessed February 4, 2023, https://www.ahdictionary.com/appropriate.
2. Merriam-Webster Dictionary, s.v. "deprive (v.)," accessed February 4, 2023, https://www.merriam-webster.com/deprive.
3. American Heritage Dictionary, s.v. "denigrate (v.)," accessed February 4, 2023, https://www.ahdictionary.com/denigrate.
4. American Heritage Dictionary, s.v. "defame (v.)," accessed February 4, 2023, https://www.ahdictionary.com/defame.
5. Oxford English Dictionary, s.v. "disdain (v.)," accessed February 4, 2023, https://www.oed.com/disdain.
6. American Heritage Dictionary, s.v. "harass (v.)," accessed February 4, 2023, https://www.ahdictionary.com/harass.
7. American Heritage Dictionary, s.v. "subjugate (v.)," accessed February 4, 2023, https://www.ahdictionary.com/subjugate.
8. American Heritage Dictionary, s.v. "recover (v.)," accessed February 4, 2023, https://www.ahdictionary.com/recover.
9. American Heritage Dictionary, s.v. "restore (v.)," accessed February 4, 2023, https://www.ahdictionary.com/restore.

REFERENCES

Hughes, Geoffrey. *An Encyclopedia of Swearing: The Social History of Oaths, Profanity, Foul Language, and Ethnic Slurs in the English-Speaking World.* Armonk NY: Sharpe, 2006.
Jacobs, Renee. "Iroquois Great Law of Peace and the United States Constitution: How the Founding Fathers Ignored the Clan Mothers." *American Indian Law Review* 16 no. 2 (1991): 497–532.

Appendix A

An Inventory of Features Template

Group A: Time, History, Ancestry

1. Time						
seasonal activity cycle						
seasonal habitation cycles						
prescience (foresight)						
dreamtime						
2. Tribal history						
notable people						
notable events						
notable places						
3. Ancestry						
ancestral lands						
ancestral identity						
ancestral beings						
ancestral scents						
ancestral symbols						

Group B: Cultural Beliefs, Values, Events, Traditions

4. Religious beliefs and practices						
beliefs about the Creator						
cosmic coherence						
spirit helpers, guides, protectors						
spiritual travel						
supernatural powers						
visions						

praying and prayers						
sacred offerings						
sacred songs						
sacred objects (miscellaneous)						
medicine bags						
spirit bundles						
sacred drums and drumming						
honoring the dead						
purification practices						
5. Cultural values						
expressing gratitude						
valuing dreams						
valuing sharing and peaceful relations with neighboring nations						
acting calmly, humbly, and honorably						
respecting others						
6. Cultural Events						
toss and catch games						
stick and ball games						
snow snakes						
game of silence						
jingle dancers						
harvest, thunder, and moon dances						
hoop dance						
grass dance						
fancy dance						
winter gathering dance						
traditional songs and singing						
special celebratory event feasts						
naming feasts						
strawberry festival, maple festival, and corn harvest						
spring festival						
celebratory dance						
Lakota naming ceremony						
Choctaw wedding ceremony						
Inuit wedding ceremony						
Sto: loh becoming man ceremony						
Indigenous coming-of-age ceremony						
7. Cultural Traditions						
traditional knowledge about local wildlife						
traditional skills: outdoor fire-making						
traditional roles						
large game hunting						
rabbit hunting						
bird hunting						
snaring						
trapping						
fishing						

clamming						
whaling						
herding						
tracking						
plant and wild rice harvesting						
water travel						
snow travel						
infant travel						
stealth						
traditional houses						
traditional shelters						
house and shelter building						
boat building and repair						
net making						
tanning						
traditional clothes						
traditional clothing accessories						
blankets and blanket making						
mats and baskets						
wood carving						
beadwork and quillwork						
tattooing and embroidery work						
toy making						
traditional implements						
traditional weapons						
traditional materials						
traditional foods						
traditional drinks						
traditional medicines						
food preparation						
food storage						

Group C: Language, Storytelling, Family Life, Kinship

8. Language use, stories, & storytelling						
ancestral language						
names and naming						
storytelling time						
the art of storytelling						
stories about the Creator						
stories about culture heroes						
stories about legendary individuals						
mythical stories						
stories about animal tricksters						
evil being stories						
eagle stories						
personal stories						
family stories						

widely circulated stories of contemporary renown						
Indigenous writing						
9. Family Life and Kinship						
extended family households						
sibling care						
sibling avoidance						
closeness to cousins						
childbirth						
childhood play						
coming-of-age experiences						
courtship						
arranged marriages						
respecting one's in-laws						
clan membership						
extending kinship to strangers						
kinship with local animals						

Group D: Destruction & Restoration

10. Divestments, Denigration, Subjugation, Disease						
material appropriation						
forced relocation from homeland						
forced removal from homeland			.			
forced separation of children from parents						
forced sterilization						
material deprivation						
cultural denigration						
disdain						
ancestral identity concealment						
harassment						
subjugation						
brutality						
smallpox						
diabetes						
11. Sovereignty, Defense, Leadership,						
sovereignty						
defense of sovereignty						
defense of homes and homelands						
clan mothers						
chiefs						
councils						
elders						
societies						

12. Restoration and Recovery						
recovery						
restoration						
cultural pride						

Appendix B

An Inventory of Features for Two Novels

Group A: Time, History, Ancestry

1. Time	TPY	WG
seasonal activity cycle		
seasonal habitation cycles	✓	
prescience (foresight)		
dreamtime		✓
2. Tribal history		
notable people		
notable events		
notable places		
3. Ancestry		
ancestral lands	✓	✓
ancestral identity	✓	✓
ancestral beings	✓	
ancestral scents		
ancestral symbols		✓

Group B: Cultural Beliefs, Values, Events, Traditions

4. Religious beliefs and practices	TPY	WG
beliefs about the Creator	✓	
cosmic coherence		
spirit helpers, guides, protectors	✓	
spiritual travel		
supernatural powers		
visions		

praying and prayers	✓	✓
sacred offerings	✓	✓
sacred songs	✓	
sacred objects (miscellaneous)	✓	✓
medicine bags	✓	
spirit bundles	✓	
sacred drums and drumming		✓
honoring the dead	✓	
purification practices	✓	
5. Cultural values		
expressing gratitude		
valuing dreams	✓	
valuing sharing and peaceful relations with neighboring nations		
acting calmly, humbly, and honorably	✓	
respecting others	✓	
6. Cultural Events		
stationary games		✓
toss and catch games		
stick and ball games		
snow snakes		
game of silence		
jingle dancers		
harvest, thunder, and moon dances		
hoop dance		
grass dance		✓
fancy dance		✓
winter gathering dance		
traditional songs and singing	✓	✓
special celebratory event feasts		
naming feasts	✓	
strawberry festival, maple festival, and corn harvest		
spring festival		
celebratory dance		
Lakota naming ceremony		
Choctaw wedding ceremony		
Inuit wedding ceremony		
Sto: loh becoming man ceremony		✓
Indigenous coming-of-age ceremony	✓	
7. Cultural Traditions		
traditional knowledge about local wildlife	✓	
traditional skills: outdoor fire-making		
traditional roles	✓	
large game hunting	✓	
rabbit hunting	✓	
bird hunting	✓	
snaring		

trapping	✓	
fishing	✓	✓
clamming		✓
whaling		
herding		
tracking		
plant and wild rice harvesting	✓	
water travel	✓	
snow travel	✓	
infant travel		
stealth		
traditional houses		
traditional shelters	✓	
house and shelter building	✓	
boat building and repair		
net making		
tanning		
traditional clothes		
traditional clothing accessories	✓	
blankets and blanket making	✓	
mats and baskets		
wood carving		✓
beadwork and quillwork		✓
tattooing and embroidery work		
toy making		
traditional implements	✓	
traditional weapons		
traditional materials		
traditional foods	✓	✓
traditional drinks	✓	
traditional medicines		
food preparation	✓	
food storage	✓	

Group C: Language, Storytelling, Family Life, Kinship

8. Language use, stories, and storytelling	TPY	WG
ancestral language	✓	
names and naming	✓	
storytelling time	✓	
the art of storytelling		✓
stories about the Creator		
stories about culture heroes	✓	
stories about legendary individuals	✓	
mythical stories		
stories about animal tricksters		✓
evil being stories		

eagle stories		✓
personal stories	✓	
family stories	✓	✓
widely circulated stories of contemporary renown		
Indigenous writing		✓
9. Family Life and Kinship		
extended family households	✓	
sibling care		
sibling avoidance	✓	
closeness to cousins		
childbirth		
childhood play	✓	
coming-of-age experiences		
courtship		✓
arranged marriages		
respecting one's in-laws		
clan membership		✓
extending kinship to strangers		
kinship with local animals		

Group D: Destruction and Restoration

10. Divestments, Denigration, Subjugation, Disease	TPY	WG
material appropriation	✓	
forced relocation from homeland	✓	
forced removal from homeland		
forced separation of children from parents		
forced sterilization		
material deprivation		
cultural denigration		✓
disdain		
ancestral identity concealment		
harassment		
subjugation		
brutality		
smallpox	✓	
diabetes		
11. Sovereignty, Defense, Leadership,		
sovereignty		
defense of sovereignty		
defense of homes and homelands		
clan mothers		
chiefs		✓
councils		
elders	✓	✓

societies		
12. Restoration and Recovery		
recovery	✓	
restoration	✓	
cultural pride		

About the Author

Don K. Philpot is a teacher, teacher educator, and writer. He is the co-author of the critically-acclaimed bilingual children's picture book *The Move, kā-āciwīkicik*, selected as a finalist in the category of Illustrated Book for Young People in the prestigious Governor's General Literary Awards 2022 competition in Canada. He is the author of three books in the Reading Actively series published by Rowman and Littlefield Publishing Group including *Collaborative Explorations of Character Experience: Reading Actively in Middle Grade Language Arts* (2021), *Reading Actively in Middle Grade Science: Teachers and Students in Action* (2020), and *Reading Actively in Middle Grade Social Studies: Teachers and Students in Action* (2019). He is the author of the groundbreaking book *Character Focalization in Children's Novels* and numerous works of conventional and experimental fiction for children and adults including *Assignments, The Moons of Goose Island, Numbering, The Victorian House, Formations & Lines*, and more.

He received his doctoral degree in language and literacy education from the University of British Columbia in Vancouver and specializes in the areas of reading pedagogy, children's literature, children's literature stylistics, and disciplinary literacy. He has been actively involved in K–8 education for four decades and is currently a member of the Reading Faculty at Shippensburg University where he teaches courses on reading comprehension, content area literacy, children's literature, reading instruction for English language learners, and most recently American Sign Language.